BUSTER
AT THE
GATE

A Golden Retriever's Heavenly Adventure

BY BUSTER
WITH HELP FROM ROGER W. HITE

Buster at the Gate
© Copyright 1995 Roger W. Hite

Date of first printing November 1995
Tobias Press

For information address Tobias Press,
P.O. Box 1890, Santa Cruz, CA 95061-1890.

ISBN 1-881591-13-1

Editing: Ted Benhari
Design: Scott Moran

DEDICATION

To Henry Rink, Roger's Mentor
And Hero. . .Who recently met his Maker.

CHAPTER 1

The towering eucalyptus trees sway gracefully in the afternoon ocean breeze, their leaves rattling as they play their
part in the summer symphony. It is one of the things I enjoy most
about my dog life on the Monterey Bay. Whether you're a dog or
a human, when you grow old here you become a philosopher.
Why? Because it's impossible to believe that all this beauty and
dynamic nature is accidental and without design. And if it is a
part of some "Grand Scheme of Things," as my human Roger
says, then even humans eventually grow curious about the Maker
of things. The more humans open their eyes to this magnificent
coastline, its crashing surf, the rolling fog banks, the early dawn
beach peacefulness, the windswept, majestic cypress trees, the
low-gliding pelicans, and the eternal ebb and flow of the tides,
the more humans search for knowledge about why they have the
good fortune of being here and not somewhere else.

People come from around the world and photograph everything. Once, when I was with Roger on the famous 17-Mile Drive,
I heard a Japanese man say to his wife from behind the camera
that seemed glued to his face, "Look. Look out there. It's so spec-
tacular! It's like we're standing before the gate to Heaven!"

I asked Roger what the man meant. I didn't see any "gate."
And I didn't have the slightest idea at that time about the place
humans called "Heaven." Roger laughed and told me, "What he
means, Buster, is that this place where we live here on earth is so
beautiful that it's the next best thing to being in Heaven with
God."

We didn't talk anymore that day about Heaven and its gate.
Both of us were too caught up in the awesomeness of the sunset.

We didn't need to say anything. It would have been sacrilege to interrupt the sermon of the sunset in the great cathedral of our coastline that evening. I knew there would be other times when I could ask about Heaven and its gate. Little did I know that someday I'd see the real thing for myself. That's what this story is all about. Did I simply dream it from my place here in the afternoon sun? Did it really happen? Am I really here on the deck? Are you reading a story told by a dog spirit? Perhaps I should just tell the story and let you be the judge...

Where we live is truly breathtaking. But the splendor is not just how it looks. It's the full experience of how it sounds, and feels, and tastes. It takes more than the lens of a camera to appreciate the grandeur of our home. The rugged California coastline south of San Francisco is where I lived with my humans Debby and Roger for the past twelve years. Even though my sight was dimming, I still savored the richness of a summer afternoon. The gusting winds that rattle the leaves seem somehow synchronized with everything else that is pulsing, flowing, crashing, smelling, screeching, surging, humming, buzzing, fluttering, and being all around me. Even though I lay comfortably in the warm afternoon sun, I often imagined I was sitting in a great music hall, like the one I've seen on the television. I imagined I'm watching and listening as some invisible conductor waves a baton and directs all the "stuffness of beingness" that Roger said is the musical score of the Grand Scheme of Things. I loved the deck of Debby's house, especially when the sun was warming my golden-white body. I loved watching the birds come to the feeder, and the squirrels scramble and play hide-and-seek around the thick trunk of the Monterey Cypress that leaned against our deck.

Sometimes I watched Bosley, our cat, stalk an unsuspecting sparrow. Usually I barked or coughed if it looked like he was getting too close. Sometimes he got mad and pranced off down the stairs to the yard below. Other times, he gave up and found his own seat near the orchestra pit as well. He also appreciated the symphony. Or, maybe he just enjoyed the sun. Either way, I liked the little purring noise he made as he curled next to me in the afternoon sun.

It was easy to lie half-asleep and listen to the endless crashing of ocean waves against the silent, unprotesting sand. Occasionally an especially loud one distinguished its moment in time. The following three of four cycles then seemed to mute their parts, until another wave established its importance in the Grand Scheme of Things. There was a time when I could see the line that marked where the horizon met the ever-changing colors of the ocean, because the line of sight to the ocean from our deck is only about a quarter of a mile. Now I relied primarily on my senses of sound and smell to experience the beauty of the coast. And I'm not complaining. Now I experienced more than when my vision was sharp. The air that washed up against our deck still had a crisp, salty smell and taste, with a little bit of fishiness mixed in for flavor. I still heard the cries of gulls. I heard the pounding surf. Robins and sparrows sang their solo parts. Dogs barked in the distance. Children shouted game rules, protested violations, and issue parental-like directives as they played in the street in front of our house.

Getting old and facing the final ending of this symphony was something I'd given a lot of thought to at that time. Even though I couldn't imagine things ending, I already felt things were indeed changing for me in how I perceived them. Roger said the older humans get, the more they change the ratio of how their senses perceive. Young humans think beauty is found in how things appear to the eye. Old humans listen more to sounds; they become educated to the languages of taste, and touch, and smell. They sharpen the vision of their mind's eye and use it to replace their dimming vision. The same thing is true for dogs.

When humans find the ratios of their senses changing, they worry about how much time is left before they die. Dogs are not as preoccupied with *it* as humans are. When Roger and I wrote our first book, "Buster at the Wall," we described the conversations we had during our walks to the sea wall that was just down the street from our house. One of the things I learned from my philosopher human, Roger, is how preciously humans regard life and how much they dread death.

One day I heard that my friend, Bo Diddley, a feisty old Bull-dog, became so old his humans finally had to "put him down." When I asked Roger if Bo had "gone to meet his Maker," he equivocated. He appeared unsure if the Creator of the Grand Scheme of Things included dogs in the place called "Heaven." I was at once both angered and puzzled. How could Heaven be the wonderful place humans believe it to be, if humans couldn't be with their dogs? It was at that moment I started worrying about *it*, just like humans do! I didn't want *it* to happen to me before I clarified what *it* was all about.

Unfortunately, like many humans, I soon found out that *it* just happens, whether we are ready for *it* or not. When it finally happened, though, it was so different from what I imagined from my talks at the wall with Roger. It happened to me in the middle of the night when both Debby and Roger were asleep.

I think we all knew my time was near. Debby had taken me to the vet just three days earlier. I couldn't help groaning as she boosted me into the front seat of the Blazer. Every bone ached with age. Once we were in the truck it was fun to sit next to Debby and nuzzle against her shoulder. We listened to one of Debby's favorite Country and Western tapes. It was a good trip. It was a simple pleasure. Simple things usually have an enormous capacity for holding pleasure.

Aging is such an interesting thing. It just catches up with us, despite how active we keep ourselves, or how health conscious we are about our food and drink. Aches and pains creep in and soon become so natural to our everyday experience we hardly remember a time when we didn't ache and have stiffness. I don't remember the day when I "got stiff." Our bodies just wear out quietly. Maybe that's a blessing in disguise. Unless we are struck with some catastrophe to our health, those of us who live a loving life, and simply wear out our bodies, never notice what is happening to us.

Once Roger told me about a dead poet named William

Shakespeare. He described what he called the "ages of man." I think he also was including "women," but in Mr. Shakespeare's time men thought only men were really important in the Grand Scheme of Things! Today, some theologians think only humans are important in the Grand Scheme of Things. (Boy, are they going to be surprised when they finish reading this story about how things really are!)

Mr. Shakespeare said humans go through seven distinct ages, beginning with infancy when they are helpless and "mewling and puking" at their mother's breast (like Spencer, Debby's baby nephew). Mr. Shakespeare described the final stage as one in which humans are "sans eyes, sans ears, sans teeth, sans everything." Roger told me sans means "without." Someday I'm going to ask Roger to tell me more about Mr. Shakespeare's mark. I was beginning to know about the meaning of "sans everything."

It had been some time since I was able to see things clearly. I was at the point where I was only able to see frosty, fuzzy images of things. Roger and Debby were worrying about my stiffness and my pain in walking. They also were worrying about my lack of bladder and bowel control. Recently I'd had a couple of very embarrassing moments, if you know what I mean. But my eyes were getting "sans" as well. I heard the vet mention to Debby that I was growing some bumps on my eyes called "cataracts." Judging from her tears, I knew Debby thought cataracts were "bad bumps."

That's not the way I saw things. The bumps on my eyes just meant that I had to think a bit harder and imagine how the trees and the roadway, the houses, and the cars looked as we drove along in Debby's Blazer. The bumps on my eyes certainly didn't diminish my appreciation of the Aptos summer symphony. I usually enjoyed it with my eyes closed, anyway!

The drive to the vet's office was so familiar I could imagine it with my eyes closed. I always liked trips to the vet. They were special times to get out and about with Debby. Age had really slowed me down. When Roger and I went to the beach wall at Rio del Mar, we no longer walked the half mile from Debby's house. We drove. And Roger finally stopped being such an old fuddy-duddy about letting me ride in the front seat of his Buick, although he still draped the seat with a big piece of denim cloth. Roger didn't even mind giving me a little boost into the seat. Humans become very gentle and caring about old people, and old dogs. I noticed how careful and polite Roger was as he helped his mother, Nadine, get around. When dogs get really old, especially dogs that are loved by their humans, they get almost as much attention as Debby's nephew, baby Spencer, did when he was three months old. Being really old has some definite benefits, especially if you are loved by your family and friends.

When humans and dogs get old, much of what they talk about are their aches and pains, their medications, and their trips to the vet. Listen to me babbling on about my health issues! There really isn't much difference between humans and dogs in the Grand Scheme of things, is there? The vet said my joints and muscles were not working well because of some kind of Latin disease. I thought he was wrong because I've never known any Latin dogs! It didn't make any difference to me what the vet called my condition. I called it "getting old." I didn't especially like knowing there was a name for what was wrong with me. I didn't feel as special, knowing that my disease could be described in precise medical terms, and that millions of other dogs had the same condition. I preferred to call it "Buster's Special Old Age Disease." That sounded really dignified and tailor-made. It took me a lifetime to create the symptoms of the Latin disease. Why not give me some credit for what I'd accomplished? But that's not the way medical science treats humans or dogs.

It made Debby feel bad, knowing that there was a special Latin name for my disease. When the vet first told her, she cried. Fortunately, my vet knew something about human feelings. He knew that Debby had raised me since I was seven weeks old. He knew we had spent more than a decade together and shared a lifetime of experiences. He also knew what to do when he had something to say to her about my disease that was not appropriate to say in front of me. He put his arm around her shoulders and walked her into the alcove next to the examination area. He spoke in a soft whisper. I heard Debby gasp and start sobbing. I think the vet must have used the "P" word—"put-down."

Debby told the vet she would think about it. She didn't think it was time yet. If they had bothered looking around the corner, they would have seen a smile of relief spread across this Golden Retriever's face! It wasn't time, as far as I was concerned. I was glad Debby had enough sense to let things take their natural course. I didn't have the slightest notion, though, what that would be. The vet gave Debby some pills to mix with my dinner meals. He told her it would relieve the pain I experienced when I walked. This time he didn't even scold me about being too heavy. Instead, he reached into a drawer next to the examination area and found a "cookie" dog biscuit. I was shocked. He patted me on my head and stroked my coat. I carefully, but quickly, extracted the morsel from his hand before he came to his senses. I should have known that my time was shorter than I thought. But I didn't. I just trotted out of the office behind Debby like I'd done for the past decade.

When we left the vet's office, I sat close to Debby in the Blazer so she could hug me. I could tell she was sad. It was difficult to tell her how happy I was that she was sad at the thought of having to put me down. If she had been calm and smiling and goody-goody about things, I would have been suspicious. But Debby couldn't hide her feelings. Even though I couldn't see her as well, I could still smell whether she was happy or sad. I could smell she was sad. I licked her face a whole bunch and distracted her while she was driving. I know ordinarily it wasn't a safe thing to do, but this time it made her laugh. I tried to remind her how I behaved as an ill-mannered and untrained puppy. I think she got the message. I made an effort to jump lively from the truck and scramble to the front door ahead of Debby, just like when I was younger.

When Roger returned from work that evening, Debby wasn't home. Roger was already dressed in his University of Oregon sweats, so I knew he'd stopped by the track on the way home for a run. He was so predictable in his behavior. I met him in the garage as the automatic garage-door yawned open and prepared to swallow his golden Buick.

"Hey, Buster, what's the good word?" Roger said as he stepped from the car. He knew the ritual by heart now. It had taken me several months to train him. He walked to the shelf and pulled a yellow tennis ball from one of the plastic containers. I headed to the new driveway of the house that was built on the hill. Roger tossed the ball in a looping arc. The ball bounced several times and began rolling down the concrete driveway. I moved as quickly as I could and neatly snatched the ball as it rolled down the hill. It wasn't exactly the style and panache I used in my heyday as a Golden Retriever, but the same feelings flowed through my old body. I crunched it firmly in the corner of my Retriever smile. I turned and looked for the outline of Roger's image. It was dark, but the backlighting from the garage allowed me to see him standing there with hands on hips. I brought him the ball. Without any game playing, I dropped it at his feet. Roger was surprised. I made no effort to keep it for myself, as I usually did. I played it straight and rewarded him forthrightly, for doing it right.

I must have impressed Roger, because instead of heading into the house and the downstairs shower, Roger stopped at the leash rack next to the garage entrance to the house and removed the retractable leash.

"Hey, mule-kicker, how about taking a walk to the beach wall tonight? We've got a full moon so the ocean should be beautiful. What do you think?" I liked it when he called me "mule-kicker." It was the term of endearment he and his friend Norm invented as their special salutation. I think I was the only other person who enjoyed the honor.

Without hesitating I moved to the passenger side of Roger's Buick. What really surprised me, though, was how Roger opened the door and boosted me into the front seat. He didn't even bother putting the denim drape over the seat. He simply shut the door and made his way around to the driver's seat. A few moments

later, we were in the parking lot next to the beach wall at Rio del
Mar.

Instead of taking our seat at the special place on the beach
wall, Roger attached a leash to my collar and we walked slowly
down the promenade toward the cement boat. A lot of people
were walking their dogs because the weather was warm and the
moon was resting high above the muted surf.

I really enjoyed such short walks. They were especially fun
ever since Roger and I wrote "Buster at the Wall." The book
made me a sort of celebrity among dog owners. Many now recognized me and called me by my name. Roger said it proved that
dogs were just like humans and enjoy what Mr. Warhol said was
everybody's entitlement to "fifteen minutes of fame." I certainly
received more than my fifteen minutes' worth. In fact, shortly
after we published the book, I had a special imprint made of my
paw so I could stamp my "signature mark" into the inside cover
of the books people bought at my grooming place, Shampoochez.

A bunch of people came a few days before Saint Valentine's
Day and bought books. I asked Roger why people celebrate Saint
Valentine's Day. He told me the holiday was the time humans
enjoyed celebrating love between people. The owner of
Shampoochez felt it was also appropriate to use the day to celebrate the love between dogs and humans. I agreed. I thought
dogs should be a part of the Valentine's Day celebration because
we are the true role models for unconditional love. Maybe we
should even have a special day called Saint Bernard's Day to cham-
pion dog love? Roger thought I was pushing things a bit with
such a notion.

For some strange reason, we both savored the walk to the
cement boat. I wondered if we both were so tuned with the Grand
Scheme of Things that we knew it would be our last walk. When
we got to the boat, a strange thing happened. Instead of turning
around, as we normally would, Roger stopped.

"Buster, how would you like to walk to the end of the cement
boat?" I looked over at the "No Dogs Allowed" sign. I could no
longer see the printing, but I could tell the sign was still there.

Roger saw my head turn toward the sign. "Oh, come on. We've always obeyed the rules. It won't hurt anything if we go out there just this one time. Besides, I think the park ranger is gone by now. Come on. You'll see some stuff you've never seen from our spot on the wall."

Roger tugged my leash gently. He didn't have to provide much encouragement. I was curious about the huge decaying hulk of the cement boat. Usually, Debby and Roger tied me to a post and told me to "stay" whenever they walked out on the boat. It even seemed like the aches and pains of my joints went away momentarily as we ventured along the dog-forbidden deck of the old cement boat.

About halfway down the deck, there is a wire fence that prevents people from falling off into the eroded lower decks of the boat. I could hear seals and sea-lions barking as we peered into the surf below. A lot of seagulls seemed to nest and hang out in the carved-out interior of the old ship. I couldn't see why there was a rule about no dogs on the ship. Roger said it was because the park rangers were worried that dogs would fall over the sides and drown in the surf. That seemed like a very lame excuse for a rule, if you asked me. At some point creatures have to assume responsibility for their own safety. I was extra careful as Roger and I walked back along the deck to the promenade. I always thought there was something mysterious or special about the deck of the boat. I found out there really wasn't. It was a very uneventful, uninteresting place to walk. It was much better, I thought, to have something declared off-limits. When things are outlawed or forbidden, that really makes them attractive! When we don't know about something, it's a lot easier to make it fearful or romantic, depending upon our perspective. When I don't know about something it's my nature to romanticize about it rather than develop fearful images. I suppose that's the way the Grand Scheme of Things meant Golden Retrievers to view things.

When we finally seated ourselves at our regular place on the sea wall, I snuggled close to Roger. The moment seemed extra special, but neither of us knew why. We sat silently for a few moments and simply absorbed the sights and sounds of the endless ebb and flow of the surf. Then Roger spoke:

"Well, Buster, what do you think all this stuff means?"

I wasn't sure I heard what Roger said. "What do you mean?" I asked.

"You know, Buster. We've been coming here for so many years. Do you think it makes any difference in the Grand Scheme of Things that we've made this journey?"

I nuzzled against Roger and licked his face. "It certainly made a difference to me, Roger. It still does."

"But have you learned anything about all this stuff that helps you as you get really old?"

I began to get Roger's drift. "Do you mean am I more prepared to meet my Maker?" I asked matter-of-factly.

Roger squirmed a bit. He wished I hadn't been so blunt. He hesitated and nervously cleared his throat before he answered.

"Well...yes, I suppose that's what I'm really asking."

I sat and thought about it for a long while. It really was an important question. Roger was very aware of how I had slowed down recently. He needed to know that I was preparing to deal with the reality of my health.

"I've learned one thing for sure, Roger. This Golden Retriever enjoys life, even when it is slow and filled with physical discomfort. When it is time for me to meet my Maker, I'm ready. The more important question is, are you and Debby ready for me to meet my Maker?"

Roger got the philosopher look on his face. Sometimes he regretted teaching me such a philosopher's gambit!

"No. We aren't, Buster. We really aren't. You are so much a part of our lives that I can't imagine not having you here with us." Roger's eyes were about ready to start running. I did my best to comfort him.

"Wait a darn minute," I joked. "You never told me that I couldn't still somehow be here with you and Debby after I met my Maker. You told me it was a real mystery about what happens when we meet our Maker. Maybe it's possible for you to feel me, even though I'm with my Maker?"

Roger thought about what I said for a few moments. Then he grabbed me with both arms and surrounded my hundred and thirteen-pound body with both arms and gave me a huge full body hug! It felt great!

"You know, Buster, I believe you're right. We will still feel you here and communicate with you even when you are with your Maker. I think you're right. Come on, let's go find Debby."

When we arrived home, I was pleased my sense of smell had not failed me. A wonderful aroma was coming from the kitchen. I recognized it immediately. Debby was home and had prepared my special meal in the microwave. It smelled gourmet. I could hardly wait to get up the stairs. Debby always prepared my meal, and Bosley's, before she prepared the food for Roger and herself. It used to bother Roger, but tonight he didn't even tease Debby about serving me first.

It was ten o'clock before Debby put Bosley in the garage and turned out the light. I dragged my blanket into the bedroom and found my customary place along her side of the bed. Roger and Debby sleep in a platform bed that has a water-mattress. When I was a puppy, Debby let me jump up on the bed. It's been years since I've been athletic enough to make the leap. Sometimes when Roger was out of town, however, Debby struggled and helped boost me up so I could sleep in Roger's place. I haven't done that for a couple of years. But I remember how good it feels to fall asleep next to Debby.

It happened shortly after I fell asleep. It didn't feel like somebody was strangling me or that I'd been poisoned. There was no struggle, nor spasms. I didn't even sense that my breathing or my heart stopped. Nothing went black. I didn't see any tunnel of light. All the stuff Roger told me people wrote about near-death experiences didn't seem to be what it was like at all. So how did I know I was dead?

I realized that I was standing atop the platform bed. There was no way I could have jumped that high. I knew instantly that the transformation had occurred. My dog spirit and soul just seemed to "unsnap" from my body. I looked down at the floor next to Debby. There I was...or I should say there was the old body that used to contain me. It was motionless on the floor. But I wasn't. I felt like a puppy. I scurried around atop the bed and bounced around between Debby and Roger. They were fast asleep and oblivious to the fact that I'd made the transition we all feared so much.

It was still me, but I didn't have any body. At least it didn't seem like I had a body. Then it occurred to me. I was what Roger called a ghost. I was curious about what a ghost might look like as viewed from the perspective of a ghost. There was only one way to find out. I bounded across the lump of covers containing Roger's sleeping body, and raced down the stairs to the full mirror hanging on the bedroom door.

"All right!" I exclaimed as I gazed into the mirror. It was me exactly the way I imagined I was supposed to be. I wasn't a puppy. I wasn't an overweight, white-coated old Golden Retriever. I was exactly the perfect calendar dog image of a Golden Retriever. I wonder if that was the way I really was, or if it was only the way I wanted to see myself. "Wait a minute," I thought to myself. "I'm sounding too much like Roger. What difference does it make whether I 'really' am something or not? When you're dead, it really doesn't make any difference whether things are 'real' or not. They seem to be the way we want them to be."

I raced back up the stairs to wake up Debby and Roger so I could show off my new form. I bounced back atop the bed and began licking Debby's face. She kept sleeping, although a funny smile came across her face. I knew she was feeling me, even though I was a ghost and she was asleep.

I licked Roger's face. He was snoring and all it made him do was turn over. But it did seem like licking made him aware of me. That was a great relief. It wouldn't be much fun being dead if I couldn't still feel some connection to Debby and Roger. Just to make sure I could still make my presence known, I burrowed down in the bed covers between Roger and Debby and started licking Debby's feet. I heard her laugh out loud. It was fun to hear her laugh. I continued to lick her feet. She finally made such a fuss, I heard Roger wake up enough to say, "Debby, wake-up. Turn over. You're snoring." Debby responded without waking up fully, as she rolled over on her side.

I decided I better stop messing around or they would both wake and find my old dead body. Then they would get upset and not get back to sleep. I'd heard about how grumpy Roger was at work when he didn't get a good night's sleep. I was curious what I would look like when they found me in the morning. I bounced down to the floor next to my old body. It seemed strange to be outside my old body. It looked so peaceful. Out of respect for the many years we spent together, I gently licked the old body's face, and helped pull the blanket over the body so it wouldn't get too cold.

I looked around the room. Here I was, dead and so full of life and energy, and with a calendar dog body and no place to go. Then I remembered what Roger told me about Heaven and my Maker. Now that I was dead, it seemed like I was entitled to find out about Heaven and the famous dog-maker God that Roger and I talked about on our journeys to the beach wall. Then it occurred to me. Maybe Roger was right. Maybe only humans went to Heaven. After all, there didn't appear to be anybody or any signs that I was supposed to follow to the place humans called "Heaven." If I couldn't get to Heaven, then it was for sure that I would never "meet my Maker."

Part of me wanted to wake up Roger and tell him how dogs seem to be excluded from Heaven. But I knew if I woke him, he would start worrying about how he and Debby were going to deal with my dead body. He wouldn't have time to answer my questions. Instead, I began searching around for a way a dog in my condition could get to Heaven.

At first I felt silly. Maybe all the stuff about Heaven was just a fairy tale humans created to ease their fear about living and dying. I caught myself in my own reasoning. After all, the human religious story about Jesus and God talked about an afterlife. Here

I was, looking and feeling like a calendar cover Golden Retriever. I had already started enjoying what Roger called the "afterlife." So if that part was true, wasn't it probable that the other part about Heaven and the dog-maker was also true? Then I looked at the doorway to the bedroom. In all my excitement I failed to notice the Door of Light the first time I rushed downstairs to look at myself in the mirror. It was there, as real as my dead body lying on the bedroom floor next to Debby's side of the bed. It felt like my heart was pounding, even though I knew that I no longer physically had a heart. I still imagined sensations as though they were real. Then I realized that things didn't have to be real when you are dead. Feelings are the only real things when you are dead. That was my first lesson as a dog spirit. And, as I was about to learn on my journey, feelings are everything.

I jumped onto the bed and licked Debby's face for one final time. She smiled. I thought I heard her say, "Have a safe trip, Buster. And come home soon." It was probably my imagination, but as I turned to give Roger a final licking for a while, I also thought I heard Debby say, "I love you, Buster."

Roger woke up when I licked his face. He sat up in bed. It startled me so much that I jumped down from the bed and stood next to the Door of Light. I'm not sure he actually woke up, but he did rub his eyes with both fists. He could have been still asleep. It didn't really matter to me. If Roger was still dreaming, fine. I just wanted to communicate with him before I left on my journey. I think Roger must have caught a glimpse of the light door because he seemed to know what was happening.

He rolled out of bed and walked around to Debby's side of the bed, rubbing his eyes all the while. I wondered if I was just being a part of his dream, if ghosts could appear in dreams where things seemed real. I had a lot to learn about how ghosts and humans communicated. When he saw my body on the floor he looked all around the room, searching for something. His eyes stopped racing and they fixed on me as I stood next to the Door of Light. I heard him whisper, "I see it, Buster, I see the light. That was you licking me when I woke up, wasn't it, you old mule-kicker? I know you're over there. I sense it. Now go and make the visit. Keep in touch and let me know if we are right about the Grand Scheme of Things. Go, Buster. Bring it back to me, Buster, bring it back." Roger walked back to his side of the bed, crawled in and returned almost instantly to a deep sleep. It was as though he were sleepwalking. He'd probably think it was all a dream when he awoke in the morning.

I knew Roger couldn't see my great Golden Retriever ghost form. He could just sense the presence of my spirit. I was sad when I realized he'd never see my perfect form. He only knew me as an old Retriever. But, then, I'd never seen Roger in his prime, either!

I looked over at the Door of Light and felt excited about my journey. I raced headlong into the light, determined to retrieve for Roger the truth about Heaven, the Maker, and the Grand Scheme of Things!

CHAPTER 2

"Oh, my God! Roger! Roger! Wake up! Something's wrong with Buster. He's not breathing! I think he's dead!" Debby shook Roger's shoulder as he opened his eyes. Even though I wasn't there physically, I was very aware of Debby's distress. Being dead allowed me to be aware of everything. I was no longer limited to the physical boundaries of what I could see or hear or touch.

Roger sat up and wrapped his arms around Debby. Her shoulders were heaving in uncontrollable sobs. As Roger held Debby he started to recall what he thought had been a dream. He remembered the Door of Light and getting out of bed and finding my body. He remembered sensing my new form and urging me to go through the door and find out the truth about the Grand Scheme of Things. I didn't like seeing Debby so sad, but it pleased me to realize that somehow I was still connected with Roger and Debby. I didn't know how it was possible, but I was about to find out a lot of stuff was possible that didn't make sense. When you're dead, things don't have to make human sense.

I was surrounded by a tunnel of light and moving forward to somewhere I'd never been before. It was reassuring that I was still connected to Debby. In my mind's eye, I could see everything happening on Wixson Street. It was unlike what Roger called the "out-of-body" experience because I knew that I would not be able to snap back into my old body. I knew I was on my own, sans body! It was comforting, even exciting, to realize I was able to retain my own ideal self-concept. There were no mirrors in the tunnel of light, so I could not catch a glimpse of my calendar dog

Golden Retriever image. But I remembered what I saw in the bedroom mirror. I didn't mind a bit that I was out of my body for good. It was worn out. I didn't miss the bumps, the hot spots, the flab, and the arthritic joints. My self-awareness was no longer encumbered with the old aches and pains of my one hundred and thirteen-pound house.

It was a good feeling, being out-of-body. I imagined how joyful newly dead humans must feel, being liberated from their old shriveled-up white-haired bodies. I was guessing, but in the out-of-body afterlife experience, everybody—humans as well as dogs—probably got to see themselves in their ideal form. I imagined that some grossly obese people must really be happy to die and have their first out-of-body experience. When they died they could be the way they wanted to appear. For people who struggled with poor body image all their lives, the new self-concept must be Heaven in itself! But I was sure that there would be more to Heaven than just ideal self-images.

My awareness focused again on Wixson Street. Debby was beside herself. She was hysterical. She couldn't believe I had died so suddenly. I was there only a few hours earlier. Now all she had was a lifeless body spread out across the carpet next to her bed.

She pulled herself from the comfort of Roger's arms and raced around the bed to where my body lay on the floor.

"Oh, Buster. Don't leave me! Please, Buster. Wake-up." She shook the old body as if she hoped she could shake it back to life.

"Please, God, don't let it happen! Not now. I'm not ready for this yet. Please, make him come back to life. Please, God! Please!"

She cradled the head of my old body into her lap and began rocking back and forth and gently stroking the head of my body. I didn't like being so aware of Debby grieving. I wished I could turn around and reoccupy the old body so she could enjoy more human time with me. I knew, though, it was my time to make the transition. I knew, too, that in the Grand Scheme of Things, it was a blessing she would now not have to make a decision to put me down.

I wished at that moment that I'd been capable of digging a hole in the back yard and burying the old body like a bone so Debby wouldn't have to find it. But things happened so quickly after I discovered the Door of Light, I forgot to think about her feelings.

Debby continued to pray to her Maker. At first she pleaded with him to bring the old body back to life. After a while, she changed her prayer. She began to ask God to protect me and to keep me safe for her until we could be together again. She asked Him to take good care of me in Heaven. I thought that was a more reasonable request of the Maker. That was what I wanted as well. I knew, though, that even the greatest, most kind, most gentle Maker could never take as good care of me as Debby did. But it was nice to know that Debby was making arrangements for a suitable replacement!

When you first die, you become very aware of which humans and dogs really like you. Even though you are not physically present, you are still aware of things. Don't ask me how. It's one of the great mysteries that does not translate well into human understanding. I learned how to appreciate that nothing is really "real" when you are dead, except feelings and awareness about being. Humans who are still alive can't possibly understand how someone can be there even though they are not perceived as "real."

I began to think about all the stuff I left behind in reality, like my blanket, my bones, my stuffed animals, and of course my leashes. None of that stuff was any longer real—it was just a part of my feelings. Did I miss any of it? No. I really didn't. What I missed about reality, though, was making my "mark." I couldn't imagine that in the afterlife there wasn't some way a dog could continue to mark stuff along the journey. I had to admit, though, I didn't have an urge to make any marks in the tunnel of light. It didn't seem right. I hoped that when I arrived at my destiny, I could make some kind of mark. I couldn't imagine how someplace could be called "Heaven" if dogs couldn't make marks!

I could not detach myself from what was happening back on

Wixson Street. Debby was working herself into a frenzy. She squeezed the old body so tightly I was glad that I no longer occupied it! Fortunately, my old friend Bosley, the cat, finally wandered into the room to see what was happening. He approached Debby and caught her attention. He was meowing because he was hungry. He didn't have any understanding of what had happened. He just knew it was after his normal feeding time, and he wanted some attention. Debby startled him as she snatched him from the floor and held him close to her tear-soaked cheeks.

"Bosley, Bosley. Buster's dead. Your brother's dead." Bosley looked down at the dead body. He didn't seemed to be terribly impressed, one way or the other. He just wanted his share of attention. He meowed two or three times very loudly as Debby held him tight and stroked his furry body. Ordinarily, I would have been offended at his lack of respect for the circumstances. But when I saw that he was distracting Debby from her non-stop grief, I was pleased.

Debby stood up, cat in arms. "Come on, kitty, I know you're hungry. Let's get you some food." She left my old body on the floor and carried Bosley into the kitchen.

Roger breathed a sigh of relief. He'd done his best to comfort Debby. He was always respectful of her efforts to communicate with her Maker, but he didn't believe the Maker was going to answer her petitions. He also knew something Debby didn't. He'd awakened in the night and experienced my new-found presence and sensed that I'd jumped through the Door of Light and was on a journey to find out what Heaven was all about. He was pleased to see that Bosley could help bring Debby momentarily out of her grief as she attended to another one of her loving animal relationships.

Debby made her way out of the bedroom toward the kitchen. Roger patted her on the shoulder and said, "It will be O.K., Debby. It's O.K. Buster's alright. I'm sure he's in a peaceful place."

Roger followed her into the kitchen. After she'd fed Bosley, he convinced her to go downstairs and take a shower.

As she headed down the stairs, he shouted down at her. "I'll take care of moving Buster's body."

Roger took a couple of minutes to slip into his Oregon sweats. I sensed he had a pretty healthy attitude toward the whole thing. But he had the advantage of knowing, or at least believing, that he'd seen me jump into the tunnel of light. He knew it wasn't just a dream. Roger believed my journey was real. He was excited about it, even though he wasn't sure how we'd communicate about the whole thing.

Roger looked down at the dead body. He scratched his head. He wasn't quite sure how to get it downstairs. I remembered how reluctant Roger had been, until most recently, to pick up my haunches and help boost my bottom up so I could get into the Blazer or his Buick. Now here he was, faced with the problem of getting a hundred and thirteen pounds of dead dog weight down the stairs. I was proud of his decision. After struggling for a few minutes to get me to the top of the stairs, he figured out the best way to complete the task. He had a silly smile on his face as he listened to make sure the shower was on in the downstairs bathroom. When he was sure Debby wasn't around, he grabbed my body by the tail and just dragged me down the stairs, my head bumping on each stair.

It was then that I knew Roger had a good attitude about things, and would keep things in perspective in the days to come.

At the bottom of the stairs, he dragged me across the floor to the side door of the garage and loaded me into the back of the Blazer. When the body was all pushed into the back, I really looked funny. My eyes were closed, and all four of my legs were pointing rigidly toward the top of the truck. Not very elegant, but kind of funny, from the viewpoint of a dog headed for Heaven. Before Roger slammed the back of the truck, he patted me on top of the head and whispered, "Sorry, mule-kicker. I know it didn't hurt, but it sure convinced me you're long gone from this body. If you'd still been home, I know for sure you wouldn't have put up with that treatment."

When Roger returned upstairs, Debby was on the phone to

her mother, Verla. In between sobs, Debby managed to tell her mom I'd died.

"Mom, Buster died last night. We found him this morning. Roger just put him in the back of my truck. I don't know what I'm going to do. I miss him so much."

Debby and Verla talked for a long time on the phone. Speaking of time, I soon discovered that "time" is a concept that is out of place in the afterlife. Why? Because "time" is a term we use to describe the relationship of things and "real" events. There isn't any such thing as "time" in the afterlife. I found out that things don't happen in any sequence in the afterlife. There is no such thing as a second, a minute, an hour, a day, a week, or a year, from the perspective of someone living in the afterlife. Everything that is left behind, including what humans chronicle as the past, present, and future, are all lumped together and exist concurrently. It is impossible to understand what I discovered about time until you're dead. When you're living in the "forever" there is absolutely no need for the concept of time. It's just as easy to feel what's happening in real time as it is to feel what happened in the past, or what is going to happen in the future.

As I traveled through the Door of Light and felt myself moving steadily toward my destiny, I enjoyed all of the feelings and impressions and recollections of things that happened during my time on earth. I especially liked the feeling of continuing to be connected with what Roger called "all the stuffness of beingness." If humans had a better understanding of non-real time, they might not be so afraid of going to an afterlife. There was nothing fear-provoking about my journey through the Door of Light. It was quiet. It was incredibly peaceful. I didn't have to deal with anybody or anything. At one point I thought to myself that "time would tell" whether I'd like Heaven or not. But I realized that "time" was going to be irrelevant. Or, at the very least, it would be measured entirely differently.

I was surprised to discover how much I remained connected to the things I loved, even though I was traveling in the afterlife. I enjoyed knowing that the people who loved me missed me. I hoped they didn't use too much of real time being sad. What I enjoyed the most during my time in the tunnel of light was having my consciousness connected so that I could remember the wonderful times I enjoyed with those who were grieving my passing. In the afterlife, all you retain are the good feelings and memories and impressions.

People grieve because they believe that they have been disconnected to people and animals they love. People caught up in living have such difficulty letting go of things that move into the future. They want to keep everything in the present, or in the past. When we are living, it's hard to imagine how we can remain connected to things that move ahead of us into the future.

In the Grand Scheme of Things, I was moving through the light toward Heaven. Many humans were grieving because it was necessary to refocus and recenter their own lives. I wanted to shout back and say "Don't worry, everything's cool on this side. You all should be bathed in such peace." But I couldn't. Being aware of Debby's grief taught me that in the afterlife I didn't need to feel guilty, sad, angry, frustrated, or any other negative feelings I had in the real world. I didn't feel guilty that I'd moved into the future ahead of Roger and Debby. I was more interested in figuring things out and getting the message back to Roger and Debby, so they could truly look forward to the journey.

My time in the tunnel taught me that reality is based upon perception of time. When you pass through the Door of Light, you pass beyond reality. I learned to appreciate what it felt like to experience "eternity." I had no idea how long the trip would take. I learned how to feel connected to everything, my past, my present, and my future. That's why I enjoyed all the feelings I had about Debby and my friends and loved ones who were grieving. Their grief seemed to comfort me during my trip through the tunnel of light.

When I jumped into the tunnel, Roger told me to keep good mental notes on the journey so I could report back to him. I was intent on doing just that. I created a notebook in one corner of my awareness. The first impression I recorded was my awareness that traveling through the tunnel of light was very similar to what it was like to hang my head out the window of the Blazer as we headed toward Debby's mom's home in Paradise, California. I noted how humorous it was that I was actually embarking on my own trip to the "real" Paradise!

CHAPTER 3

"Arf, Arf...Wulff, Wulff...Arf, Arf...Wulff..." What a sight and sound for sore eyes. There at the end of the Door of Light was a calendar dog image of a squat, fighting-weight lean and mean Bulldog. I instantly recognized him. It was my best friend since puppyhood, Bo Diddley!

Bo trotted toward me with his cute little macho swagger. He was no longer dragging his back leg like he did the last time I saw him at Pam and Norm's house. He wasn't as fat, either. He wasn't drooling like he did toward the end of his life. His eyes were no longer cloudy and perpetually bloodshot. He looked great, better than I'd ever seen him look when he was real and alive. He was bouncing up and down and side-to-side on his muscular little legs—legs to which I always thought the Dog-Maker should have added a couple more inches. It flashed across my mind that maybe I could apply my user experience and advise the Maker on dog body designs. After all, I no longer had to protect Debby's house from strangers. And I did have a lifetime of experience operating and evaluating dog bodies. I'd certainly seen a lot of peculiar designs in my time! It was clear that the Dog-Maker had never bothered spending much time piloting dog designs!

I began clearing my mind from all of the tunnel light. Bo came over and pushed his pudgy wet nose against mine. He walked around me a couple of times, sniffing me all over. He was just as surprised at how great I looked as I was about his own robust image. Neither of us spared anything as we projected to each other our ideal images. It seemed to me, though, that Bo exaggerated a bit some of his body parts, if you know what I mean. I glanced down at myself. Well, maybe I did overdo certain aspects as well. What the heck. Now that we were in Heaven, we didn't have anything to be ashamed about.

"Sorry about the screw-up, Buster. I was supposed to meet you at the entrance to the Door of Light. It was my first assignment and I blew it. I thought I could get a couple of other things ready for you before I did the light tunnel thing. How was I to know you would be so eager to jump in all by yourself? Most creatures are reluctant to move through the door without some coaxing. That's why they send a friend as an escort."

"Hey, Bo. Don't worry about it. I was O.K. It did seem like it took forever to get here, though."

My humor went right over Bo's head. He never was much for puns and humor. Bulldogs are no-nonsense critters. It didn't surprise me that Bo hadn't changed.

"Does this mean you're what Roger calls my 'guardian angel?'" I asked, half-kidding, as I sniffed around and tried to get my bearings.

Bo followed behind me, sniffing and poking his nose around. His nose was so cold, I always jumped when he poked it into parts of my body. It was no different in the afterlife. I tried, nevertheless, to be polite and not respond. He was really excited to have an old friend join him in the afterlife. I have to admit, it was really a relief to see another familiar dog. I would have known I was at the wrong place and in "deep do-do" if I'd been greeted by my old enemy, the black cat, that's for sure!

"Well, Buster, I guess I'm something like that. We have a buddy system here, so nobody feels lonesome. I'm assigned to help you settle in and get acquainted with how things are here."

I felt like I wanted to make my mark, but I held up, not knowing whether such behavior was appropriate.

I looked around. I was surprised to see a brick wall that looked a lot like the one Roger and I sat on during our walks to the beach at Rio Del Mar. In fact, everything about the place was strangely familiar. I trotted over and sat down. Bo followed. It was a comfortable feeling, even though Roger wasn't here with me to talk about stuff. Bo was, though, and he was starving for conversation. I began to appreciate how easy it was to feel a sense of familiarity in the afterlife. Roger's going to be really excited when I tell him he can look forward to wall-sitting and thinking here. Bo and I both squirmed as we settled into comfortable positions side-by-side on the wall.

It was peculiar, but everything seemed so familiar. I smelled the fishiness of the ocean. I heard all the sounds of the coast. I recalled all of the Blazer trips with Debby to Verla's place in Paradise. I could hear baby Spencer. I could see Debby's smiling and loving face. I could feel the sensation of her brushing my golden coat. I remembered the excitement of chasing the tennis ball up the hillside next to Debby's house. I could feel how good it was to hump my blanket and play tug-of-war with Debby. As I sat on the wall with Bo I realized that Heaven was really all about being aware forever of all the good that has happened during one's life on earth. Unless I really chose to focus on one good thing, I could experience all the goodness at once. It was a wonderful sensation. It was one that would have overwhelmed my senses back on earth.

I noticed, though, that it was possible to focus on specific things if I wanted to and felt the need. I focused on the idea of the wall and I found myself sensing all that was familiar and real about the brick wall at Rio Del Mar.

Bo was tuned into my feelings. He seemed to enjoy the pleasure of my most special place. He wiggled and squirmed as he tried to find a comfortable position on the wall. He continued our conversation.

"You remember Casey, the Terrier that was in our obedience class?"

"You mean the one that was run over by the garbage truck?"

"Yeah, that's the Casey I'm talking about. Well, he greeted me at the Door of Light in the vet's office. I suppose you heard that Pam and Norm had to put me down?"

"So I heard. How did it feel? Were you worried and

frightened?"

Bo chuckled. "Nope. I was cool, but you should have seen poor Pam and Norm. I really felt sorry for them. The big guy cried worse than Pam, if you can imagine that. I was half tempted to see if the vet couldn't put them down as well, just to get them beyond their grief. What a bummer. It's no relief to give up your worn-out body and enjoy what we got now, when it has such an impact on the people you love. I wish things were a bit different in the Grand Scheme of Things. I wish people could know how much better everybody is in this afterlife. I can't imagine why people are so confused about these kinds of things."

"I can, Bo." I replied, as though I were in dialogue with Roger at the wall. "Religion."

"What do you mean, 'Religion?' What's that got to do with people being afraid of the afterlife?"

It felt really neat. There I was, talking just like Roger talked to me at the wall. I paused for a bit to think about how I was going to explain my theory to Bo.

"It's like this, Bo. Religion is often used by some humans to scare other humans into behaving the way good people are supposed to behave in the Grand Scheme of Things."

"How does religion scare people?" Bo asked innocently. I sense that he hadn't had too many discussions with humans about the subject.

"Some religions teach that if you aren't good, you won't go to Heaven. In fact, if you're really bad, you go to a place called hell where you burn in fire forever."

"No kidding? Some people actually believe that. I thought that religions were supposed to teach people about how good Heaven really is, and to prepare people and get them excited about coming here."

"Well, if that were true, how come people go to such great lengths to prolong the trip through the Door of Light as long as possible?" I asked Bo as we sat at the wall.

"I didn't know they did, Buster," responded Bo. He snorted

and cleared his throat so his voice didn't seem so gruff. He didn't have to worry, though, about me misperceiving and not seeing the puppy personality hidden behind his Bulldog's tough-guy image.

"Humans are afraid, because the longer they live, the more opportunities there are to do stuff that might prevent them from getting to Heaven. The longer some of them live, the more stuff they accumulate, so that they think they have a piece of 'Heaven on earth.' I once saw a bumper sticker that read, 'He who dies with the most toys, wins!' When humans get a lot of stuff, they feel they are in control of their little world. They often are. That causes them to lose sight of the fact that their little world is like a grain of sand, in the Grand Scheme of Things."

Bo nodded his head. He understood, I felt myself beaming as I played the part of a Roger-like philosopher at the wall.

"Do you know that Roger and Debby and your human, Pam, all work in places where people come to get fixed so they don't have to cross the threshold of the Door of Light any sooner than necessary?" I asked Bo.

Bo looked over at me and smiled. When Bo smiles it almost splits his entire head into two parts. He was sitting on the wall next to me, just like I did when Roger and I made our walks to the beach. He nodded his head from side to side, and gazed off at stuff I still couldn't see very clearly.

"When some people get so sick and old, and in pain, they and their families often say it's O.K. for the vets to put them in hospital beds and hook them up to all kinds of fancy hoses that are poked into their noses, their mouths, and connected with needles to all parts of their body. One of the hoses is sometimes used to dump their food right into their stomachs so they don't even get to enjoy smelling it, chewing it, tasting it and swallowing it."

Bo's eyes got really big as he listened to my description.

"Why do they do all that?" he asked. "It sounds like a description of the kind of 'hell' they are afraid they will go to in the afterlife."

I chuckled. "You've got my point exactly, Bo. Some humans

become so fearful of going to the afterlife, they are willing to put up with great pain and suffering. In fact, there are only one or two places in America where humans can even think about 'putting down other humans.' In most places, regardless of how much suffering is occurring, it's against the law to consciously put down humans. Many religions also teach that it is bad."

"What other alternatives do people have, if they can't put down other suffering people, or if they don't have the right to ask their vet to put them down?" Bo asked.

"Roger told me humans in the hospital can ask that no extraordinary means be used to keep them alive. They can also ask and expect to have everything done so that they are as pain-free as possible when they are experiencing the final days of their worn-out bodies. But they can't ask their vet to put them down. That's not legal. And that's not moral, according to many religious codes."

From the tone of Bo's voice, I could tell he was agitated. I could see he was offended as he thought about what I implied about Pam and Norm, the humans who took him to the vet so he could be put down.

"That sounds kind of dumb to me. How come it was O.K. for Pam and Norm to put me down? What does the law and religion say about putting down dogs?"

"Roger told me that the law says it's O.K., because there are rules set up by the SPCA, that's the Society for the Prevention of Cruelty to Animals. It says that animals can be euthanized to put them out of pain and suffering. As far as human religion is concerned, it tells humans to be kind to animals. Some religions evolved out of a tradition of using animals as a sacrifice to God. So I think some animals don't matter as much to some humans as others. At least that's what I got from talking to Roger about the early religions. He also told me there were other human religions where it was O.K. to sacrifice humans to please the Gods, too. So there's always been a lot of variety in how human religions have valued human life and human suffering.

My comments about animal and human "sacrifices" really

stirred Bo's interest in human religions.

"You mean some religions actually said it was O.K. to kill animals and some humans, not just to put them out of their pain, but because they felt it made God-the-Maker happy?"

I realized I was going to have to explain myself in more detail, so Bo didn't get the wrong idea about religions.

"Let me put it in another way, Bo. A long time ago, primitive religions taught humans that they were subject to the whims of things from the afterlife called spirits, angels, demons, and gods. If a person wanted to live a life that was not fraught with pain and suffering, if they wanted their crops to grow, and their herds to multiply, and their wealth to accumulate, they were taught by their religions to do things to keep the Gods happy."

"But I thought God was the Creator of all things, including animals?"

"That's what our humans believe, Bo."

"Well, how come it didn't make God angry that humans were killing some of his creatures?"

"Interesting point, Bo. I'm not sure. But I think what the humans believed was that they owned the animals. And it was a 'sacrifice' for the humans to give up the best animals from their herd in honor of God."

"How did they do the sacrifice?" Bo asked.

"According to Roger, they burned the dead body on an altar. Roger said some of the priests in the ancient tradition ate the meat after it was sacrificed."

"Did they ever sacrifice dogs?" Bo asked hesitantly.

"No, I don't think so. In fact, it was just the reverse among some of the ancient Egyptian religions. Some of them believed the dog was a special creature that sat next to the rulers on the throne. They also worshipped images of certain dogs. But I never heard of dogs being sacrificed. They usually used 'the fatted calf,' lambs, and some kinds of birds."

"How come the human religions finally stopped sacrificing animals?" Bo asked, as he scratched his jaw with his hind leg. It always made me smile when I saw him do that. His legs are so short that he gets a contorted look on his face. But it must be worth the effort to relieve the itch.

Why did they stop? I had to think about that for a while, until I remembered what Roger told me about the Christian religion and the Grand Scheme of Things.

"There are a whole bunch of reasons, Bo. Now most humans don't have their wealth tied up in large herds of animals. They have money and bank accounts. Now the churches ask that humans sacrifice part of their wealth. It's called a 'tithe.' The money that is sacrificed by people is used by the church to help the other humans created by God who need help. That's one reason."

"Another reason is because something great happened about two thousand years ago, in earth time. The Christian religion began among the Jewish tribes. The religion was founded after a human named Jesus Christ was sentenced to death by hanging on a cross. When He died, He didn't come immediately here to the afterlife. Instead, He stayed near his friends. Then, after three days He appeared to them. He said that He had come back to life to prove to them He was the son of God-the-Maker-of-everything. His miracle of returning from death was a fulfillment of a promise that God made to humans that He would send his Son to become a human, and to help them learn the ways that would allow God to welcome them into Heaven. He told them that if they believed He was the Son of God-the-Maker-of-everything, and if they lived a good life, He would make sure there was a place for them to stay in Heaven. The Christian religion teaches humans to worry about doing good and showing love for other humans. That's the way the person called Jesus Christ asked humans to make sacrifices to God."

"I think I'd like that person Jesus," Bo remarked. "Did He have a dog when He was alive on earth?"

I had to laugh at Bo's comment. "Heck, I don't know, Bo. I'd think you'd know the answer to that one by now. You've been here for a while, haven't you had a chance to meet guys like Jesus and find out?"

A frown appeared on Bo's broad face. He cast an intense look at me, as if I'd asked a very touchy question.

"Look over there, Buster. What do you see?"

We'd been so engrossed in our conversation ever since Bo met me at the exit to the Door of Light I'd really not paid much attention to our surroundings. I'd been made to feel at home because we found a wall not unlike the one Roger and I sat on at Rio Del Mar. I looked out and saw some magnificently ornate gates, like the ones that I'd seen on television surrounding the huge mansions of the really rich people.

I heard myself gasp at the beauty. "Wow," I exclaimed. "Is that Heaven?"

Bo shook his head up and down. "Yep. That's it. The one and only. Those are what the humans call the 'pearly gates.' That's what they worry so much about getting past once they enter the afterlife. That's where God and Jesus and all the good humans live together forever."

My eyes got wider and wider as I listened to Bo. I had to keep good mental notes about what it looked like so I could somehow communicate it back to Roger and Debby, like I promised. All I could think to note was that it was truly breathtaking.

"Now that I'm here, Bo, what do we have to do to get permission to go inside the gates?"

Bo frowned. "We don't do anything, Buster."

"What do you mean?" I asked. "Aren't there some papers I sign, or some collar and documentation that have to be put on me, like the government jingling tags Pam and Debby put on us when we were on earth?"

"Take a good close look at my neck, old buddy. You don't see any collar or tags, do you?"

I examined Bo and he was right. No tags. I was curious how the Maker kept track of all dogs without tags.

"You mean we don't have to wear collars and tags in Heaven? That's great. That means they don't require leashes either, right?" I was now standing in front of the wall, anxious to go on with the journey beyond the gates.

"Hey, not so fast, Buster. You're not getting my drift. I don't

have any tags or collar because there is no need to have identification to get beyond the gates. What I'm saying, Buster, is that
dogs don't get to go into Heaven. We go over there, in that
direction."

Bo motioned with his head toward a grassy field that seemed
to appear out of nowhere. It was peaceful enough. It was dotted
with trees, and a creek ran through the rolling hillsides. As far as
you could see were open fields. As I looked, I began to see dogs
in the distance romping through the grass, lying in the shade of
trees, and playfully chasing each other as they splashed through
shallow puddles formed from the gentle mist that kept everything so green. It was largely what we remembered as our best
experiences on earth. But there were no humans. Just dogs.

"Wait a minute, Bo. Are you telling me that dogs don't get to
go into Heaven where the humans are?"

"Sorry, buddy. That's the way it is in the Grand Scheme of
Things."

I looked at the grassy, pastoral hillsides and then over at the
magnificent golden and glittering gates to Heaven. At first I was
stunned. Then I became angry. There was something terribly
wrong with this picture. How could Heaven be Heaven for Debby
or Roger or Pam and Norm if they couldn't enjoy being with Bo
and me? Then it occurred to me. Bo must mean that the dogs live
in one area and humans in another. Maybe there was a place where
we got to meet and be together.

"Let me get this straight, Bo. Do you mean we live separate
but equal lives here in Heaven? That there is a dog area and a
human area?"

Bo nodded his head, "Yes."

"O.K. That's not the way I'd design it. It certainly isn't perfect, from my perspective. But I guess that's the way it is. When
do the humans get to go over there and take us on walks and play
with us?

Bo had a real scowl on his face. He must have known I wasn't
going to like his response. He was right.

"They never get to be with us. They've got more important

things that God has them doing there in the place behind the great gates. At least that's what all the dogs tell me who've been around here for a long time."

I became really angry. I made my way willingly and eagerly through the Door of Light to this place in the great afterlife, only to discover that Roger's concerns were valid. It appeared that in the Grand Scheme of Things, there really wasn't a place for dogs.

I wanted to show Bo what I thought about the fate he just described. There was only one way. I jogged over to the great glittering gates, and began parading from one side to the other, stopping every few yards and defiantly making my mark!

Bo gasped, and couldn't believe his eyes. "Buster," he shouted at me. "Are you crazy? Do you know what could happen to you for doing that?"

"No. What?" I asked as I completed my work and returned to where Bo was standing in disbelief. He backed away from me as if he was afraid to acknowledge I was his responsibility here in the afterlife.

"I'm not sure, Buster," Bo exclaimed in relief that lightning hadn't struck either of us. You've got to calm down. It really isn't so bad here. It really isn't. Besides, there's nothing we can do about it. It's the Grand Scheme of Things."

"I'm not so sure you're right, Bo. Has anybody ever asked God-the-Maker-of-everything if that's what he intended? Have you ever seen God?" I asked Bo.

He shook his whole body as though he were drying off from some unwanted bath. "No, I haven't ever seen God. No dog has." Then it occurred to me. "Come on, Bo. Let's hang around and see how humans get through the gates. Then we'll ask whether we can have a few moments of God's time to make sure God knows how we feel about this scheme."

Bo stood his ground. "Are you sure you want to do this? I don't think I'm supposed to let you do this. I'm supposed to help you settle into the way things are here. I'm not assigned to help you change things. Nothing ever changes here. It's supposed to be perfect the way it is. Besides, God is supposed to know about everything. They'll just laugh at you when you say you want to tell God something. They'll say God already knows."

"How do you know God's a He? Maybe God's a She," I suggested to Bo as he stood his ground and seemed unwilling to join in my adventure.

"Why would it make any difference?" Bo asked.

"Maybe it does and maybe it doesn't. But one thing is for sure, Bo," I said as I headed for the gates.

"What's that?" Bo asked as he finally joined me.

"There's something that isn't perfect about Heaven from my point of view. And I won't believe it's truly supposed to be this way until I hear it from God. Heaven can't possibly be Heaven without dogs. Surely God knows that there's been some great mistake here that I've got to fix before Debby and Roger arrive."

CHAPTER 4

"Here we are Harry. What do you think?" A short, plump, balding man in an avocado green leisure suit, a gold chain around his neck and a white silk open collar shirt appeared before the gates. He had a neatly trimmed mustache, and black-framed glasses with tinted lenses. He was in his late fifties. A large diamond ring glittered on the pinkie of his left hand as he stood before the gates and spread wide his arms, as though he was selling real estate and pointing out a splendid view site to a prospective client. Beads of sweat glistened on his forehead. He was breathing heavily as if he labored greatly to bring his companion to this precise spot. His "client," though, wasn't especially awe-struck. He was still clearing his head from the journey through the light.

Bo and I were lying on our bellies, side by side, nestled tightly up against the wall next to the gates so we could avoid being discovered by the two men. Bo whispered to me, "Buster, if I were the tubby little guy I'd get with the new program. Doesn't he know he can project his ideal self-image here in the afterlife? He's about the most ordinary looking human I've seen since I've been here. I wonder what gives?"

"Hush, Bo. Not so loud. He'll hear you." I reminded Bo that his deep bass voice carried a lot farther than he realized.

"Maybe that is his ideal form. Maybe it makes him feel the most comfortable. Everybody isn't so vain about their looks. It's refreshing that he can feel comfortable looking like that, especially when everybody else has such heavenly bodies. It wouldn't be my choice either, but to each his own. Look at us. We never looked better. And look at his friend. He looks like Robert

Redford." The man called Harry rubbed his eyes and finally spoke to Murray.

"Murray, you sound like you're still selling real estate. Give me a break! You don't have to convince me. I'm ready for this place. After that rat-race and treadmill computer industry, anything will be a change for the better. I've already seen hell. I'm sure there are people already here who would tell you that I created it for them as well. God rest their souls. I'm sure leadership was cursed at more than one funeral. We all knew, though, that hell was really about trying to get a new software product to market before Microsoft. After two divorces, a five-vessel coronary-bypass, three kids, and a thirty-year mortgage, I'm ready. Trust me."

"You're going to love it, Harry. Everything's perfect. Nothing's broken. Nothing ever needs fixing or cleaning. The lawns and the shrubs are perfectly groomed. There are no noisy neighbors. The values never go down. You can have as much square footage as you need. Everybody has a mansion..."

"Murray. Cut the sales pitch. You don't have to sell me. It's been a long trip. How do we officially get me moved into this great neighborhood?"

Murray took his escort role very seriously. He stood there, looking up and down at Harry's ideal form. "You look great, Harry, I must say. You really look great. A lot better than when I last saw you in the ICU at Memorial. Boy, you look at least thirty years younger! Isn't it amazing?"

Harry took a moment and inspected himself in the full-length mirror that appeared from out of nowhere. He smiled as he turned slowly to examine the image he projected for his friend Murray. Then he realized that Murray looked just like the old Murray, the person who worshipped the Salesman-of-the-Year trophies that crowded the mantle of his fireplace in a swank suburb of Los Angeles. Murray attributed his success to his "bonding" with everybody and anybody he'd ever sold anything to during his fifty-eight-year career as a salesman. That was why Murray was with

Harry when he had his bypass surgery, years ago. Not that Murray wasn't a compassionate person, but he also thought it was good business to visit previous clients in the hospital. Oftentimes it led to listings on homes that had to be sold—either by the surviving patient who wanted to simplify his/her life—or, sadly, listings that were made by grieving widows who needed to restructure their lifestyles.

"Hey, Murray. What gives here? Look at you. You still look like a middle-aged couch-potato. Now you can look exactly as you want to look. Come on. What's with this image?"

Murray smiled and turned slowly around, as if modeling his underbelly, that draped not-so-elegantly over his belt line.

"Harry. This is me. Trust me. I know. This is how I like seeing myself. I was a fat baby. I had pimples when I was fifteen. I've been pudgy all my life. But it really didn't matter much then. And it certainly doesn't matter here. So, this is me. I'm comfortable. Besides, I discovered that it's a lot easier to get reacquainted here if people see me this way. You know, I've talked to a lot of people who have such a hard time recognizing even their own relatives. They say they've passed by them countless times on the streets without even having the slightest notion of who they are. One guy recently told me he and his wife of sixty-two years passed by each other twice before they recognized each other! During their former life, she swore to him that she liked her nose and breasts just as they were. He said he'd never get a toupee, even though he looked like a bowling-ball before he was thirty-five. I can hardly wait to see Oprah and Donahue to see how they really imagine themselves. That ought to be interesting. There's no accounting for how anyone really sees himself, now that people are obliged to face reality!"

Harry was not impressed with Murray's little cultural lecture. He paced back and forth at the gates as Murray continued to ramble.

"Now in my case, I don't have that problem. People come up to me and say. 'Murray? Murray Goldman, is that you? Aren't you the guy who sold me my first house?' I still get a thrill out of that moment, even here in the afterlife. That's what it's all about, Harry. Recognition and being remembered for doing good for people. That's what got me here. I'm convinced of it. Why tamper with a good thing? That's what I say."

"Come on, Murray. Cut the altruism. You don't need to impress me; and apparently you've already impressed the gatekeeper. You made a fortune in real estate. Now you make it sound like you were some kind of social worker. You made six percent on my two-million dollar estate! And if you were still alive, you'd be signing a listing agreement with Gladys in the parking lot of the cemetery." Harry was smiling and seemed to enjoy his perverse teasing of his friend Murray.

"So how do we get in? Is there some kind of bell we're supposed to ring? They never taught us anything about this when we went to temple."

"Hold your horses, Harry. Hold your horses. We have all the time in the world, so hold your horses."

Bo's eyes grew big when he heard Murray talk about horses. Bo hated horses. Once he got out and ran down the road from Pam and Norm's house and started barking at the heels of a horse that was boarded on a neighbor's property. The horse only put up with it for a few yips, then his left rear hoof launched Bo thirty feet through the air, and into a clump of bushes. Bo reminded me that he had not seen any horses in the afterlife. That was why he was so concerned that maybe this human called Harry might propose their entry to Heaven. I told Bo not to worry, it was just a figure of speech. He looked puzzled, so I told him to be quiet so that we didn't blow our cover, and that I'd explain it to him later.

"Come on, Murray. What gives here? Aren't you supposed to be my escort and make me feel at home?"

"Sure. Sure. That's what I'm doing. Don't get so huffy. We've got eternity. There's no reason to hurry here. Time is irrelevant."

Harry didn't seem impressed. He began searching around for some way to open the gates.

Murray did not appreciate his friend's frustration. He shook his head from side to side as he approached the gates, and he mumbled to himself. "Some people. Give 'em the royal treatment, lead 'em to the very gates to Heaven, and they're not satisfied. I think they expect me to enjoy it for 'em. Go figure. Most people are dying to get a chance to enjoy this place. But not old stick-in-the-mud Harry. He's the kind of guy who, once he's inside, he'll want to hurry up and get on with it. Boy. You've got a lot to learn about this place, that's for sure, ol' buddy."

"What are you mumbling about, Murray? Can't you find the lock-box?"

"I said, 'Boy, have you got a lot to learn about this place, Harry.' That's all."

Then, as though appearing from out of nowhere, a man, dressed in jeans and a red plaid long-sleeved wool shirt, spoke to Murray and Harry.

"Welcome, Mr. Hartman. I see your friend Mr. Goldman has brought you safely to our gates."

Harry seemed startled. Murray was relieved. Without hesitation, he spoke to the casually dressed man.

"I'm glad you finally appeared, Peter. My old friend was beginning to question our hospitality. I know you like privacy during these confidential screening interviews, so I'll be on my way." Murray turned to his friend and waved good-bye. "Good Luck, Harry. By the way, don't be intimidated by Peter. He's Catholic. He has a hard time understanding Jewish humor—but that shouldn't be a problem for you. You don't have any! I'll see you around. I'm sure. Once you get beyond ol' Saint Peter, here! Shalom." Bo and I watched as Murray just seemed to grow transparent.

While we watched amazed as Murray faded away, we didn't notice that a desk and desktop computer were suddenly in front of Peter. When we finally refocused, there was Peter pecking away at a keyboard. Harry sat with his legs crossed in a straight-backed chair. He seemed puzzled by the contradictions.

"Excuse me, Peter."

"That's Saint Peter, Mr. Hartman. We prefer to keep things

formal during these entrance interviews."

"Forgive me for being informal, Mr. Saint Peter. But you are dressed sort of casually for this sort of thing, I must say."

"It's Saint Peter. Not *Mr.* Saint Peter! Saint is my professional title. This is the only place where I'm required to use it," said the human in the red-plaid shirt. He looked over the top of his bifocal glasses and stared into Harry's eyes to make his point. Even though there was a smile on Saint Peter's face, Bo and I could tell he was quite serious about his professional business. We listened carefully to the conversation, because we knew we'd have to pass a similar scrutiny if we wanted to make it beyond the gates into Heaven.

Peter typed furiously on his keyboard and squinted to read the messages that were appearing on the screen of his computer. It was an Apple. When Harry noticed the brand logo, he decided to make light conversation.

"Hey, what a pip. Here I am, registering for an eternal stay in Heaven, and I'm talking to a Catholic saint in a red-flannel wool shirt who's typing stuff on an Apple computer. Why an Apple, if you don't mind me asking? When I was alive, I worked for IBM. Hey, what an irony. An Apple. That's what the Devil used to tempt Eve. Now you're using an Apple. Don't you see the humor?"

Harry's voice trailed off. From the look on Peter's face, he didn't find anything funny about Harry's observation.

"If you don't mind, Harry, please stop being so anxious and nervous. It always seems to happen to those who know they are marginally qualified. Relax. You wouldn't be sitting here if you weren't going to get admitted. You don't need to make feeble attempts to charm me with small talk. I've heard it all. So just relax. I just need to verify some information before we issue you a password and your Personal Identification Number. Then you can enter."

"I don't have to be Christian? I mean, after all, I'm not dumb. When a Jew appears at the Pearly Gates and confronts a Catholic saint, you can appreciate that it creates a bit of anxiety. I mean, am I supposed to tell you I'm sorry? I was wrong. Rabbi Jesus was really right. Am I supposed to sign some papers like Copernicus and recant my erroneous beliefs? Is that what this interview is all about?"

Peter continued to search his computer data bank, almost oblivious to Harry's babbling.

"Do you think you were wrong?"

"Well, no, not really," responded Harry.

"Then shut up... please. If you think you feel funny, imagine how the Buddhists, the Moslems, the Mormons, and all of the other religious 'isms' feel when they arrive. No. As hard as it is for most dogmatically religious people to appreciate, Heaven is truly ecumenical. That's just the way we are. Why do you think I dress this way? Do you think *I like* Levis and red-flannel plaid shirts? Yech! This is the way I'm supposed to communicate that things are nothing like the way the religious dogmas have portrayed us. I don't even have a set of angel wings. But I do have a 49ers football cap. God says I can't wear it, though, because at some point we'll have Dallas Cowboys coming through these gates looking for passwords, despite what San Francisco sports reporters say!" The moment Peter said "password," he'd struck a familiar note with Harry. Harry sat straight up in his chair and leaned forward, intensely interested in Peter's activities. Peter continued to type furiously at his keyboard, pausing occasionally to make note of the images on the screen.

"I'm impressed. Imagine. Heaven is computerized. I'll bet this makes your job a lot easier, doesn't it?"

Without looking away from his work, Peter responded.

"We've had computers ever since the beginning. It's nothing new. How else do you think we know about everything? It was only when things started getting complex on earth that God-the-Maker-of-everything decided to let humans discover the technology."

Harry sat back and began rubbing his chin. "Sure! It only makes sense. We're just beginning to use computers to understand stuff. I can imagine what God's been able to do with a computer designed to meet the Maker's needs. Wow. Imagine the programming. It would make the Pentium chip seem like a cow chip."

Peter interrupted Harry's thoughts.

"I've validated our data bank on your experiences. You've come to terms with the things that would not be acceptable in our experiences here." He spun the computer monitor to allow Harry to view the screen. On it were two sets of numbers.

"Please make mental note of these two numbers," Saint Peter said. The first is your access code. The second is your PIN. Have you memorized them yet?"

Harry nodded.

"Good. Now you can enter."

"What am I supposed to do once I'm inside?" Harry asked, as he stood up from the chair and turned toward the gates. Bo and I watched as the chair and the desk, and then Saint Peter himself, faded away.

Harry stood there, now talking to himself. He looked around, trying to understand what was happening. Then, as though he'd figured out some huge mystery, he exclaimed out loud. "That's what it's all about! This whole place is virtual reality. Incredible. We were just beginning to discover the power of the concept when I left the company. That's why Peter and Murray and all of this stuff seems to appear and disappear out of nowhere. Everything and anything is possible in virtual reality. It's just a way of looking at things. It's not like reality." Then Harry stopped. A peaceful smile spread across his face. He was finally ready to pass beyond the gates.

Harry put his hand to his forehead. "How foolish we've all been, probably since the beginning. We thought that reality was material and tangible, and bankable. It was acres of soil, structures, pork bellies, precious metals, and stocks and bonds. We called all that stuff 'reality.' And now we find out in the Grand Scheme of Things that reality isn't in what is material. It's in the other stuff. We've just started sniffing around on earth. I wonder if there is enough time for humans to finally know about the Grand Scheme of Things before the patterns of reality on earth come to an end?"

As he talked aloud, I heard some warm, friendly laughter coming from nowhere. It seemed to startle Harry. He stopped talking and strained to listen.

"Harry...Harry... Harry. Stop trying to figure everything out. There's nothing to figure out here. If you want to call it 'virtual reality' you can. But there is nothing unreal about virtual reality here, I can assure you. You're about to find out that virtual reality is only a small piece of the great mystery—a mystery that is not necessary to unravel now that you're here. Shalom, good person. Shalom."

Harry had a curious smile on his face as he faded from our view, presumably having entered beyond the beautiful gates.

Bo looked at me. We stood up and shook the stiffness from ourselves.

"What was that all about, Buster? What did he mean, 'virtual reality?'"

"I'm not quite sure, Bo. But we're going to find out."

"Do you think there's any stuff on Peter's computer about us? How are we going to get into the grounds of Heaven?"

"All we need is a set of those numbers that Peter gave Harry."

"How are we going to get our numbers?"

"We're going to ask Peter! Come on. Let's go over and stand in front of the gates and see what happens. That's what Murray and Harry did. Let's go."

CHAPTER 5

One of the curious things about the afterlife was how effortlessly I could go anywhere. In truth, I'm not sure we go anywhere in time or space. We just seemed to focus our awareness on stuff and it appeared and disappeared. Consciousness and awareness were instantaneous. It didn't take any time at all to find ourselves in front of Heaven's Gate. We just had to determine that's where we wanted to be. The gems created a dazzling rainbow of light. I wasn't sure I could ever tell Roger how magnificent the gates are. All the jewels and gems that were so treasured by wealth seekers on earth were embedded in the solid gold of the gates: diamonds, emeralds, sapphires, rubies, and amethysts. Bo told me that one of the reasons thieves never made it to Heaven is because God didn't want them stealing all the valuable stuff in the gates. I thought he was kidding, though, because not only can't you take wealth into Heaven, but it didn't seem like there was any way to take it away from Heaven either. Funny, though, I didn't notice any pearls. I wondered how the myth began that they were the "Pearly Gates?"

"What are we supposed to do, just sit here and look smart?" said Bo as we seated ourselves in front of the gates. It never occurred to me that we were about to make history. If all went well, the two of us would be the first dogs to ever enter Heaven. I looked at the green rolling hills that bordered the gates and wondered how many other dogs would soon flock to the gates, once we clarified the great misunderstanding in the Grand Scheme of Things. I sensed that Bo didn't share my conviction. There was a slight quivering in his image as we sat there together.

"When's this guy Peter going to appear, like he did for Murray and Harry?"

Bo needed encouragement. He'd already made up his mind. There was no way we were going to convince the gatekeeper to let us enter. I wasn't sure myself, except I knew it wouldn't be Heaven for Debby if dogs were excluded. I didn't want her making a scene when she arrived and found out that I had to stay outside the gates. She might cause a stir and get sent to the other place! Roger said Debby was a sure candidate for Heaven, so I didn't want her getting in any trouble. She was very stubborn when she wanted to be. This guy called Peter will have his hands full if he thinks Debby will enter without me. The more I watched Bo shift his weight from side to side, though, the more nervous it made me.

"Relax, Bo. I can't imagine we won't be able to straighten this thing out. After all, the guy in the red flannel shirt seemed nice enough. Didn't you hear them call him 'saint?' Roger told me humans hold saints in high regard. Some people love them almost as much as they do their dogs!"

Bo scoffed. "The only saint I've ever heard of was a big fat, drooling dog. All he ever did was slobber all the time. When he got really old, he looked like a polar bear, he was so big and white. And stupid! He gave a new meaning to stupid. Half the time when he made his mark, he'd end up dribbling all over his own feet! What a klutzy oaf."

"Really?"

"That's the honest truth, Buster. You know what was so funny? He even looked like his human."

"Really?" I didn't want to be impolite to Bo, but it made me uncomfortable to hear him talk so harshly about a fellow creature. I knew the human he was talking about. And as much as I hated to admit it, Bo was right. The Saint Bernard did look like his human!

I could tell Bo was nervous. Twice he stood up and walked around aimlessly in a circle, sniffing and pretending he was searching for something. He marked the gates once. He didn't want to; but he had to go somewhere. That often happens when dogs get really nervous.

"So, what do we have to do to make Mr. Peter in the red shirt appear?"

I only knew one sure-fire way. I told Bo. "On the count of three, let's both start howling and barking."

"You've got to be kidding. Nobody makes a fuss here in Heaven, not even over there in the hills where the dogs roam. It's not the way things are here. Nobody is noisy. I haven't barked out loud once since I arrived."

"So? You still know how, don't you?" I asked impatiently.

"Hey, just watch me."

"Well then, let's get on with it. One...two...three!" We broke into our best howling versions of, "You better let me in soon or I'll wake up the neighborhood," combined with, "If you don't let me out soon, you'll be calling the carpet cleaners!"

It worked perfectly. Even though there was no measure of time in Heaven, it still seemed that it didn't take but seconds for Peter to appear from out of nowhere. He was still wearing his red shirt and Levis. But there wasn't a smile on his face. Bo stood up and slowly backed away from the gates where Peter was standing. I could hear him growling in a low tone—trying to pretend he was brave—but ever so slowly moving to what he must have imagined was a safer place behind me! I stood my ground and presented my happiest Golden Retriever smile. Ordinarily, it disarmed anyone and usually got me what I wanted from either Debby or Roger. But Peter wasn't buying it. He frowned. His arms were folded tightly across his chest. He stared down at us with a judgmental look. Bo and I felt a cold chill bathe our bodies.

"What's going on here with you two dogs? Don't you know noise isn't acceptable here? It violates the peace. Heaven is forever peaceful. If there's something wrong in the Green Valley you know what the procedures are, Bo Diddley. You've been around enough to know how things are. Is this the new dog you escorted recently?" I was amazed that Peter seemed to know everything. But then, that was part of his job. I was sure we'd found the right person to talk with about this great misunderstanding about dogs. But I didn't know what he was talking about when he mentioned "Green Valley."

I looked at Bo. He could see the puzzlement on my face, so he whispered to me, "Green Valley is what we call the good dog place."

I nodded. Then I cleared my throat. "No, sir. There's nothing wrong with it. It looks like a great place to chase around in." I paused. I could feel my voice trembling. I swallowed several times because my throat became dry as an empty water pan in the sun.

I continued. "Sir, my name is Buster Tobias Sampson. I'm Debby's Golden Retriever. I grew old and died before Debby. You sent my friend Bo here to fetch me safely to this place. But there's one thing wrong, sir."

Peter looked over the top of his glasses down at Bo and myself. His arms were still folded, and I could tell he was impatient with the two of us.

"Wrong? What could possibly be wrong? You're here, aren't you? It's not possible for anything to be wrong. This is Heaven, the Pearly Gates, and glory land. Nothing's ever wrong here."

It was clear Mr. Peter didn't get the picture.

"Sir, I don't want to sound impolite, but how can it be Heaven for humans who love dogs if we have to stay out here?"

Peter seemed puzzled.

"Don't humans who owned dogs get into Heaven?" I asked.

Peter laughed nervously. "I certainly think so. Let me check to be sure."

Peter sat down behind his desk, which appeared out of nowhere. He swiveled around his computer and began typing into the keyboard. Bo and I watched as Peter scanned through data on his screen. He muttered to himself. "Let's see, earthly possessions. Money, property, jewels, boats, cars. Ah. That's it. Animals. Sheep. Goats. Cattle. Pigs. Horses. Dogs. Bingo! Dogs. Let's see if we can sort this stuff out."

He typed a few commands and rocked back in his chair with

his arms again folded against his chest, as he pridefully watched the computer search its files. Then he leaned forward and a smile spread across his face.

"Just as I expected. Here it is. Yes. Definitely Heaven is full of humans who owned dogs. 86.77% of everybody in Heaven owned a dog at some point in their lives. It says here we use dog ownership as a 'screening indicator.' How 'bout that. Even I didn't know that was a part of the program in the Grand Scheme of Things. You learn something new every time you learn something new."

I smiled. I shot an 'I told you so' look at Bo. His ears perked up. Now we were getting somewhere. Almost everybody in Heaven had a relationship with a dog sometime in their life. I was sure we were about to straighten things out.

Peter was intrigued by the relationship between dogs and humans. "Will you look at this? It's amazing. Look at all of the well-known people who had dogs. Moses had a Retriever. Buddha had a Retriever. So did Adam. Ghandi had a mongrel. All of the popes except one had a dog when they were growing up. Most of the presidents of the United States had dogs. Hmm. 'Checkers.' What a strange name for a dog. Dominic had a dog. Goodness. The list goes on and on. Even Jesus had a Golden Retriever puppy, the offspring of Joseph's dog. I had no idea."

"So. Don't they ever miss their dogs?" I asked respectfully.

"It's not possible to miss anything in Heaven. That's not the way it is in the Grand Scheme of Things. People have all of their needs taken care of forever."

"Doesn't anybody ever complain about anything?"

"Speaking figuratively, never. Of course, there is no such thing as 'never' in Heaven."

"Let me get this straight. If nobody ever complains in Heaven, then it isn't possible to change anything in the Grand Scheme of Things?"

Peter nodded in agreement "That's right. We would consider changing things if there were complaints. But people don't complain. Until they do, we don't change."

I whispered to Bo. "So. I came all this way to find out that the Grand Scheme is built on a classic Catch Twenty-Two."

"What's a Catch Twenty-Two?" Bo whispered to me.

"I'll tell you later, Bo," I whispered back. "It's an expression created by Mr. Heller."

"Did I hear someone say 'Hell?'" Inquired Peter, looking very stern and judgmental at the two of us. "We do not allow cursing here in Heaven. You know that, Bo."

"Yes, sir. I mean no, sir, he didn't say the bad word. It's a man's name. Heller. Joseph Heller."

"Certainly, yes. I know the name. He's on the list. Of course it's confidential. He's not passed through the Door of Light yet. We have a lot of writers who, shall we say, don't pass the 'test,' if you know what I mean. Writers have such a time of things. I must say."

Bo looked at me and whispered, "Uh oh. I hope he doesn't know you're a writer, too. Now we're going to have two strikes against us and we haven't even begun."

"Ssh, Bo. Let me do the talking." I wasn't sure how Peter was going to like what I had to say, but I knew if I didn't come up with something to say soon, Peter would fade back to wherever he goes when he's not attending the gates.

"Are you the one who made up this Grand Scheme of Things?" I asked cautiously.

"Heavens, no," responded Peter. He smiled and seemed genuinely flattered. He considered it an honor to be mistaken as the creator of the Grand Scheme of Things."

"No. I didn't make the GST…that's what we call it here. The GST. It was the work of the Creator. In the beginning is when the GST happened."

Peter was interested in talking about such stuff, so I did my best to imagine how Roger would engage Peter in dialogue. "Were there dogs in the very beginning?" I asked cautiously.

Peter put his hand to his chin and began rubbing it. I could tell he'd never thought about this question before. He didn't seem to mind the puzzlement it created in his way of thinking.

"Actually, in the very beginning, there was nothing but the Creator. So, it would follow logically that there were no dogs in the very beginning. They came later."

"All right," I thought to myself. Now we were getting somewhere. I didn't want to make Peter feel stupid, so I asked another question.

"How much later?"

"What difference does that make?" rebuffed Peter. This time there was a gruffness to his tone. "Later is so relative. Isn't it enough to agree that they came later? What's your point in all this doggedness?"

"Well, sir, I don't mean to be rude, but I'm trying to understand all this creation stuff. If dogs didn't exist at the time the Creator created the GST, then how did dogs come into the picture? Did they happen before humans or after?"

"Frankly, Buster Tobias Sampson, I'm not sure. But what difference would it make?"

"Well," I continued, "Let's suppose that there was some sequence of life that was formed. Debby told me the Bible said the Creator made everything in seven days. Now I understand that until the GST was created, there was no 'time' or 'calendar' as we think of such things in the GST. But let's suppose that everything didn't happen at precisely the same moment."

Peter nodded. "Quite possible, quite possible. Continue."

"Well, as you know, Peter, there's always been an argument among humans about this thing called evolution. Probably because we can't understand the sequence of stuff in the GST. The scientists argue that life form evolved out of life form until humans appeared. Fundamentalists don't like the scientist's view, and they think that the Creator of the GST made all of the individual creatures pretty much all at the same time, within the first week of existence."

"So, what do you think, Buster? How did it really happen?" asked Peter. I felt like I was in one of those human school classrooms I'd seen on television. Only this stern teacher called on me and I didn't even raise my hand!

"Well, sir. I think that when the Creator started making stuff, the Creator got all excited with the first type of life that happened. It was simple then. The next type of life was more complex. And finally, the Creator got so good at creating life stuff a dog was created. That was the end of the life forms that were supposed to be created in the GST. Then the Creator had a dog that would always fetch whatever was thrown. The Creator knew that the unconditional love between the Creator and the dog could not be improved upon."

Peter wasn't convinced that my theology was according to his sense of how the Creator made dogs in the GST. But at least he listened to my comments. "So, Buster Tobias Sampson..." Peter let the parts of my name roll off his tongue with such an icy, sanctimonious tone that I could hardly remain polite. But I did. And he allowed me to continue.

"Well, as the Creator played with the dog, it was apparent that there was something missing. At first there were only Golden Retrievers. Then the Creator designed a whole bunch of different types of dogs."

I looked over at Bo, who was beginning to shake his head in disbelief at the story I was telling Peter. But I figured my explanation of creation was just as plausible as the scientists' and the evolutionists'. So I went on:

"The second type of dog created was a Bulldog." I glanced over at Bo and smiled. He smiled back, and was now more interested in my explanation. I figured it didn't hurt anything to make up some details that probably weren't altogether true, but could really make some of the creatures happy. Bo didn't seem to mind that he was a descendant of the second breed created. I knew that some humans, however, didn't like the thought that some scientist thinkers reasoned that humans were created after monkeys. Being first is really important to a lot of people. And as I thought about it, it also occurred to me that it must be important to dogs as well. It made me feel special to have been the first type of dog created, whether it was factual or not.

"So, when do you think humans came along in the GST?" inquired Peter, who was now becoming engrossed in my strange theory.

"Well, it didn't happen for a long time, even though there was no way of measuring time the way humans do until humans appeared. It was a long time because the Creator got so much pleasure from all the different types of dogs created. Then, probably somewhere close to the sixth day of creation, according to the Bible's timetable, the Creator decided that it would be easier if some other kind of life were a part of the GST. That's when the idea of creating a human occurred to the Creator. The Creator decided that for every type and breed of dog it would be appropriate to create a type of human with which a dog could be put into a relationship. That's why there are all the races, and colors, and sizes and types of humans."

Bo was now getting into the story as well. He stood right next to me and said to Peter. "Yeah, Mr. Peter, sir."

"That's **Saint** Peter."

"Yes. Well, Saint Peter, that's the truth of the matter. That's why so many humans look like their dogs. That's the way it's supposed to be in the GST."

I was pleased to see Bo was so excited. It made sense to him. And it certainly made sense to me. I came to the conclusion of my story. "In the GST the dogs were supposed to teach all humans about unconditional love. Unfortunately, over the course of human history, too many humans went charging off in pursuit of their destinies and forgot to take their dogs along with them. That's why the world is so screwed up today. If every human had a dog, there would be peace in the world. That's about all I have to say about things."

"What is the point of all this, Buster Tobias Sampson? What am I supposed to do? Why are you here telling me all this?"

"Don't you see, Saint Peter, sir? There's been a terrible mistake in the GST. Humans and dogs are essential ingredients of unconditional love. A dog isn't really a dog if the dog is without a human. A human really isn't a human without a dog. It's all very biological. Humans evolved out of dogs. We're related in the GST. It isn't fair to separate us in Heaven."

"What are you asking me to do? Do you expect me to change the GST?" By this time Peter seemed like he'd heard enough. He knew where my story was going. He was standing and impatiently striding back and forth in front of the gates like some kind of sentry. I knew he wasn't about to do anything. Nevertheless, I pressed my appeal.

"Precisely. Change it and you'll really make Heaven what it's supposed to be!" There was a weak pleading tone to my voice. All of the bravado of my past few comments had disappeared. I was whimpering with my request.

Peter stopped and turned toward Bo and me. He looked me directly in the eyes and said: "And if I don't... which I can't... what are you proposing to do, Buster Tobias Sampson?"

I paused for what felt like an eternity. Then I blurted out. "If you don't change the GST, then I'm going to find the Creator and ask Him."

Peter smiled, almost unctuously, then slyly grinned at both of us as he said: "Well, Buster Tobias Sampson and Bo Diddley, that's going to be a bit difficult, wouldn't you say, inasmuch as the Creator never goes outside the gates." Then he disappeared, leaving Bo and me sitting staring at the great gates.

Bo tried to console me. He knew I'd given it my best shot, and I think he was proud I'd made a case for dogs and humans together. "Come on, Buster," Bo said, as he turned and headed for the hillsides outside the great gates, "Let me introduce you to some of the dogs in Green Valley. It's not a bad place."

I stayed and looked at the gates. I knew it was only a matter of a few human years and Debby and Roger would be arriving. I didn't have much human time to get this thing fixed.

CHAPTER 6

When Peter left us at the gates, he went immediately to
visit the Creator. All we could do was wait until Peter returned. Bo suggested that we take a nap. I agreed. During that
nap a curious thing happened. I became aware of everything that
Peter was doing. It was as though I had the ability to visualize
things that were important to me. I couldn't make myself present
with Peter and the Creator, but I could listen in on their conversation. In the afterlife there are no secrets. Nothing is confidential. Something is either your business, or it's not. If it's not, you
are not aware. If it is, you're aware. The Creator must have known
that such phenomena wouldn't work on earth.

Peter was anxious as he entered the Great Temple. As I
watched Peter in what I imagined was a dream, I was aware of
the splendor of the magnificent temple. It was bigger than any
building I'd ever been in with Roger and Debby. I wondered
who built it. Did the people who went to Heaven have to build
stuff? Did it build itself? Did the Creator build it unassisted? It's
funny how difficult it was to shake myself free of such earth-bound
practical questions. As my journey continued, I became less and
less logical and discerning of how or why things worked the way
they appeared in the afterlife. The temple was filled with thou-
sands of people. Unlike what Debby told me about church ser-
vices on earth, everybody seemed like they really wanted to be
there. Roger once told me one of the primary reasons some people
go to church was to pray that God will let them enter Heaven. So,
what would those people have to pray about if they actually arrived in Heaven?

Peter hurried through the temple so that I didn't have a chance to let my awareness linger and study the people worshipping. Once things were straightened out in the Grand Scheme of Things, I'd be able to visit the place with Debby and Roger.

As we passed through the worship area of the temple, I was struck by the realization that there was no pulpit. Nobody was preaching anything. In Heaven there was no longer any need for words or theology or scriptures. Here, the worship engaged all of the senses to their fullest level of awareness. When the Creator finally decided to create humans, the "word" was created. The word was a special gift the Creator gave humans, and not dogs, so humans could talk and converse about the meaning of the unconditional love that bonded them to their dogs. Unfortunately, the word was so powerful it enabled humans to create views of realities that didn't actually exist. When humans mastered the use of the word, they found that saying something was so, seemed to make it so. It was possible to draw word maps of territories that didn't exist in reality. The word enabled humans to create all kinds of curious religions and theologies and beliefs. The word was at the core of all earthly troubles. The people in the temple were not worried about the meanings of religious words. They were no longer divided by the words of their various earthly theologies. Perhaps that was why I felt a great sense of peace as Peter hurried through the temple.

Peter felt the powerful energy flowing throughout the presence of everyone in the Great Temple. He was so preoccupied with the special problem Bo and I'd created through our presence at the gate that he absorbed very little of the good energy. He knew he would want to return soon for his own sake.

Finally, Peter's awareness focused on the presence of the Creator. A great sense of peace enveloped him like the warmth of sunshine I experienced lying on the deck of Debby's house in Aptos. The Creator has the special ability to appear in forms that would not overwhelm visitors. I was curious how Peter imagined the Creator. If I didn't know better, I would have sworn that Peter

watched some old Hollywood epic films. His image of the Creator was fresh from a movie set. Peter imagined the Creator had
magnificent angel wings, a well-groomed blond beard, pearly
white teeth (not the rotten ones that afflicted most men of Peter's
time), and long golden blond hair that wasn't oily and dirty, like
that of most men Peter mingled with during his apostleship with
Jesus. He imagined a golden aura encircling the Creator's head.

He pretty much viewed the Creator as depicted by
Michelangelo on the ceiling of the Sistine Chapel. This image
was not the Creator's favorite, but He knew Peter's preference.
So, with the exception of the wings, which the Creator decided
He would never use, He stood there in front of Peter and greeted
him with outstretched hands.

"Peter, My friend. It's good to see you. Please, come and sit
with Me." He approached Peter and embraced Peter's shoulder
with one arm as He led him toward a private conversation pit.
They stepped down into the circular pit and seated themselves
on the soft cushions. The Creator sat back, spread His arms out
atop the cushions behind Him, and patted them gently.

"So, what's on your mind, Peter?"

"Well, sir. It's about what happened at the gates with the two
dogs."

"You mean Bo Diddley and the new arrival, Buster Tobias
Sampson?"

"Yes. I know you're aware of the incident."

"Yes, I am. What is it that is bothering you? I think you handled
it quite nicely."

Saint Peter fidgeted in his seat. He still had difficulties accepting compliments. His Catholic heritage made him more comfortable with guilt feelings than with acknowledgment of his suc-
cesses.

"Thank You, Sir. You're most kind. I am not deserving of Your
praise. But I willingly accept it. My concern is about what the
dog Buster Tobias Sampson said, Sir."

"What about it, Peter? I thought it was rather well spoken."

"Is it true?" The Creator smiled and again patted the top of the cushions with the palms of His outstretched hands. He seemed almost amused by Peter's innocent question and his obvious concern.

"I think it is a true statement of Buster's understanding of the Grand Scheme of Things. Yes. Buster is telling things truthfully, from a dog's perspective."

Peter didn't want to contradict or seem disrespectful of the Creator, but the answer didn't satisfy him.

"Sir, with all respect. I would like to know more about how things happened when You first implemented the Grand Scheme of Things. Did You actually think You were done with creation when You made dogs? And did You make dogs before You made humans?" The Creator enjoyed Peter's questions, and He understood completely what was going on in Peter's mind. He chuckled aloud and leaned forward, His hands folded between His knees. His voice was almost a whisper as He looked into Peter's eyes. Peter could see the twinkle in the Creator's eyes—but he didn't understand the reason for the look.

"Peter, My friend and colleague and confidant. I'm going to let you in on little-known information about the Grand Scheme of Things. Throughout human time so many scientific theories and religious theories have developed to explain the beginning of time and the origin of the species. Most of them have a bit of the truth, but some miss it altogether."

"Yes, I know. I understand that now humans are being told by some scientists that the whole cosmos was created by a big bang. Isn't that a silly little theory?" The Creator smiled and rubbed His bearded chin as He appeared to contemplate the theory.

"Well, actually, I can understand why some think that way. You see, the instant I conceived of the Grand Scheme of Things, it all happened virtually simultaneously. Remember, the GST happened before there was any such thing as time. And there was no such thing as space or matter either. They were what scientists now call fractals of the GST. They were My essential ingredients. The moment I created matter it needed space. It was necessary, then, to create a cosmos amount of space so matter could move toward its perfect design. So, it simply appeared like an explosion. And because it is continuing toward its destiny, toward the perfect design, it takes what humans refer to as time and it appears to be expanding constantly."

Peter listened intently. He wasn't sure he understood what all this explanation had to do with humans and dogs. The Creator continued. "When I created all the matter I also created the possibility of life. And in My GST life didn't explode like the universe, but it happened naturally and systematically. From the human perspective, I understand why some think all creatures were created in a few days of human time. And I also understand why some think creatures evolved from one form into the other. It's all a matter of human perspective."

Peter interrupted. "Yes, that's precisely my question. The Buster dog says You created dogs and were satisfied at that point. And that humans were created as an afterthought, to provide companionship and love for dogs. Is he right?" The Creator folded His hands together beneath His chin and leaned forward as He whispered to Peter. "Yes!"

Peter was startled with the simple response. He didn't know what to make of it. Now that he knew this truth, what was he supposed to do?

"I don't understand, sir. Are You saying that in the GST humans were an afterthought? That You were satisfied when You created the dog?"

"Exactly. You remember how in the Jewish scriptures they write about the genesis of things and how the book describes the garden?"

"Yes. The Garden of Eden, I think they called it. Was there really such a place, or was that just another simple metaphor so humans could visualize a beginning place for life to begin?"

The Creator smiled. "Oh, it was an actual place. In fact, it still is."

"It is?" Peter asked as his eyes grew wider. Where is it? I've never seen it."

"Peter, Peter. Open up your mind's eye. It's the dog's place, the place outside the gates. It's the place we call Green Valley. That's the original Garden of Eden. It's the one pure place where I first created the ideal home for dogs."

"I had no idea. Amazing." Peter shook his head in disbelief as he contemplated the simple truth the Creator bought to his awareness. The Creator continued his story, sinking deeper into the cushions. "It was My favorite place; what I envisioned as the ending point of creation. I still remember My own awe as I fashioned the first dog. It was what humans now call a Golden Retriever."

"You mean one that looked like this Buster Tobias Sampson who appeared at the gates?"

"Yes. A magnificent creation, don't you think?"

Peter nodded his head in approval, although he really hadn't ever judged the merits of a dog. It wasn't a part of his judgment responsibilities.

"So Buster was right about the creation of dogs? How did he know?"

"Simple. It's part of his innate knowledge. What humans call his genetic signature. Apparently this Buster dog has become quite the thoughtful, introspective creature. Once he evolved into a philosopher, it was only a matter of time until he became aware of the truth."

"Incredible. This Buster dog can trace his existence back to the original dog in the Garden of Eden? Incredible. What a coincidence that Buster is now at the gates wanting to be admitted."

"Oh, it's no coincidence, Peter. That's the way it's supposed to happen. He's a key part of My GST."

"Does that mean I'm supposed to let him in?" asked Peter haltingly. He was thinking about how he'd have to develop some new admission criteria, and process the millions and millions of dogs that were currently enjoying the afterlife in Green Valley.

"Not yet, Peter. Not yet. It isn't at the right point yet. Things still have to happen in My GST."

"What am I supposed to tell Buster and his companion, Bo,

when they come again and start barking at the gates?"

"Tell them they must retrieve the Gospel of Sampson. The gospel reveals what has to happen before dogs can live with humans behind the gates. The change Buster wants will not happen until the Gospel of Sampson is fulfilled. It's all part of the GST." The Creator was through talking about me and Bo. He changed the focus of the conversation to something that was more pressing to Him.

"Enough talk now about Buster Tobias Sampson," He said. "Let me tell you what I'm really excited about. Harry has arrived."

"Harry?" inquired Peter, trying to imagine which Harry the Creator was speaking about. You can't mean Harry Hartman?" The Creator nodded. "Yes. He's the one. He holds one of the key pieces to completing the Grand Scheme of Things."

"He does?" inquired Peter, who was still reeling at the thought of dogs coming into Heaven at some point. He'd heard about our habits of leaving marks on everything. It was hard for him to imagine that God's design included such a habit.

"Yes. One of the most wonderful things about the Grand Scheme of Things is that it is distributed among all humans. Each is born with a unique role and part to play in the GST. All humans possess a unique piece—a gift, as the humans call it. Some gifts are more critical than others, but humans are not aware of anything about the importance of their unique gift. Sadly, some are not even aware that they have any special thing to contribute."

Peter nodded. "Yes. I know. I've turned several of those poor souls away at the gates. They never seem to make the connection. What a tragedy."

"Yes, it is *the* great tragedy," replied the Creator.

"But let's celebrate the positive. As people return to the gates, they bring their parts back together into the wholeness of the grand scheme. When all of the critical parts are brought here, it will be possible to complete the grand scheme."

Peter smiled. He knew the full story. "I know. That's when

the human world is brought to an end and things go back to the beginning in Heaven."

"That's right, Peter. But I don't think I told you an important thing about My GST. When I distributed the gifts among humans, I didn't design any special order in which the gifts would return to Heaven. I just determined that they would. I also didn't keep track of who received which gift. I would become aware of the gift as it was manifested in the things I saw happen in the course of individual lives." The Creator smiled, as though there were an inside bit of humor He was about to share with his colleague, Peter. He continued. "You see, Peter. I designed into the GST a surprise factor for Myself. It's My way of keeping things interesting for Me. I don't know from, arrival to arrival, what pieces are coming together. Each arrival brings the grand mystery closer to completion. But I don't know when it will actually happen. But I can tell you, Harry is really an exciting arrival!"

"Why Harry?" asked Peter, who was finally shaking the dog problems from his own awareness.

"Let me show you," responded the Creator, as they found themselves in a huge room filled with people intensely involved in activity. It resembled the central information processing center of a mammoth corporate headquarters. In one corner, a group of men and women were gathered around Harry, who was sitting at a computer console, explaining something theoretical to the rapt crowd.

As they watched from a distance, the Creator spoke in a soft voice to Peter. "Harry's gift was in theoretical computer sciences. His company was a pioneer in virtual reality technology. Harry has brought some new understanding to the Revelations Project."

"You mean the one that was written about in the human's Bible?"

"Precisely. We need a systematic way to instantly de-matterize all of the matter that was originally programmed in My GST to return to the beginning. Now that the cosmos has expanded for such a time, and there is so much space and matter, we're having a hard time programming its return. But Harry's new information is hot stuff. I can tell from the excitement I see on the faces of the others. I sense it won't be long before we can engage the Revelations Project. Then you're going to have to add staff at the gates. We'll have to really scramble when everything returns that's supposed to return."

Peter still couldn't get images of me and Bo out of his mind. He knew he was going to have to deal with us again very soon. One thing still disturbed Peter's understanding of Green Valley and the story I'd told him at the gates. At the risk of appearing less bright than he wanted to be in the mind of the Creator, Peter again brought the subject back to my story.

"Sir, there is still one thing that puzzles me."
"You mean about the original Golden Retriever dog?"
"Yes."
"You wonder why I created humans? It was very easy. I wanted a creature that could enjoy the pleasure and the love that comes from a relationship with a dog. The creation of humans was a perfect way to create a constantly growing energy field called love. The plan was to have each dog give love to its human. Then humans were supposed to learn how to give this same kind of love to other humans. The more dogs, the more humans, and the more love. That was one of the design features of the GST."

"O.K. I understand that, but what went wrong? How did dogs get so separated from humans in the GST, so much so that they are not currently allowed to be together in Heaven?"

"Part of the story is written in the Jewish scriptures. In the beginning, after I gave the first two dogs their humans to play with, everything was perfect in the Green Valley. Then one day, instead of picking up a stick and throwing it for the Golden Retriever to fetch, one of the humans picked an apple from the forbidden tree of knowledge. The human threw it and the Retriever fetched it. As the Retriever placed the apple ever so gently in the side of its mouth, it bit into the apple just enough to taste a few drops of the forbidden fruit's juice."

"What happened then?" inquired Peter.

"In an instant, all of the knowledge of the GST became a part of the dog's awareness. When he returned, instead of giving the apple to the humans, he knew that they were not supposed to taste the fruit because it was forbidden by the Creator. The dog was aware of My existence, but humans were not. All the humans wanted, though, was to get the apple from the mouth of their Retriever. They had no understanding of why he refused. It wasn't long, however, before they became frustrated and angry with the Retriever. One of them took a stick and struck the dog, forcing him to drop the apple before their feet."

Peter gasped. "You mean they struck the dog for no apparent reason, except their own frustration?"

"Yes. It happened. The first non-loving act. It was at that point I appeared and ordered the humans to leave Green Valley. I told them they could not expect to enjoy the unconditional love and devotion of dogs until they had practiced loving other humans. I told them that when they finally learned how to love other humans as their dogs had loved them, then I would allow humans and dogs to be linked in the eternal GST."

Peter shook his head. "So, it wasn't the woman who was tempted by the evil spirit that was the cause of all the subsequent suffering and grief experienced by humanity. It wasn't the woman who ate of the tree of knowledge. It was the first Golden Retriever?"

"That's right. Only an ignorant human would ever hit a dog. It was the hitting of the dog that created ignorance in humans. It was eating the apple that made the first dog aware of the unconditional love he had for the human. The dog still licked the hand of the human who hit him with the stick."

"Was it the Evil One who caused the human to hit the dog with the stick?"

"Not quite. There was no Evil One, until the moment the stick hit the dog. It was that act that occurred in the GST that was not a part of the plan. It was, shall we say, the original mutation. It was that act that created the possibility of further non-loving acts. To prevent non-loving acts from occurring in the future in Green Valley, I simply commanded the humans to leave. It wasn't until later that I began to see the pattern of evil acts grow. And each non-loving act contributed to an evil force. Over time, the force became very powerful. That's why I'm a bit anxious to get on with the Revelations Project. Judging from Harry's work, it will come about soon.

"Well, sir. I must say this has been an extraordinary afternoon. I'd best return to the gates. I'm sure I have a couple of dogs waiting for my return."

"Peace be with you, Peter."

"And also with You, Sir."

CHAPTER 7

"Wake up, Buster! Wake up!"
Bo was poking me with his hard wet nose. I finally opened my eyes. I hated it when he poked me that way. But as soon as I saw it was him, I realized that at least it was a friendly nose. I yawned, and stood up to shake off the drowsiness of my nap.

"Come on, let's go over to Green Valley. I don't think Peter's ever going to return," Bo said.

"Yes he is. The Creator told him to come back here to us. I dreamed about it. I was there when Peter spoke with the Creator. At least it seemed like I was there. Heavenly dreams are sure different from earthly dreams."

Bo looked at me like I was crazy. Just then, however, Peter reappeared at the gates. I smiled knowingly at Bo. He shook his head in disbelief.

Peter wasn't surprised to find me and Bo at the gates when he returned.

"Good, you're both here. I need to talk with the two of you. I've just come from a visit with the Creator. And I've got a message for you."

I looked at Bo. I didn't want to tell Peter that I knew about his conversation with the Creator. I tried to look surprised.

Peter sat down in his chair and seemed to be a bit fatigued, as though he had just returned from a very long and tiring journey. It also might have been a sign of the heavy burden his new knowledge had placed upon his shoulders.

"I spoke with the Creator about your concerns."

"And did he agree that it was not really in the Grand Scheme of Things to have dogs separate from humans?" I asked, already knowing the answer.

Peter shook his head from side to side. "No. In the Creator's GST there is a design for why humans are separate from dogs. It goes way back to the beginning of human time."

I sputtered. "What? You mean that Heaven is supposed to be Heaven without dogs? Impossible. With all respect, sir, I don't believe that's what the Creator said. I feel in my whole being things are supposed to be different. Did the Creator tell you that it was true that dogs were created before humans? Did the Creator tell you that humans were only an afterthought in the GST?"

Peter didn't hesitate to agree on that point. "Yes. He said that in the beginning He created two dogs. In fact, the first was a Golden Retriever. You are a direct descendant of that first Golden. I think his name was Sampson."

I wasn't as surprised as Bo to hear Peter confirm what I believed all along about dogs. We were the Creator's chosen creatures. That's why our special gift is the ability to give unconditional love.

Bo nudged my side with his nose. "Buster. Ask him about the second dog. What was it? Please."

"Mr. Peter, you said there were two dogs in the beginning, and one was a Golden. What type was the second dog?"

"That's Saint Peter."

He could see the anticipation on Bo's face. To not disappoint him, Peter hedged his answer. "I'm not exactly sure. It's quite possible it was a Bulldog, but I can't be sure."

Bo responded instantly to Peter's feigned uncertainty. "Come on, Peter, either you know it or you don't. It really doesn't make any difference to me. I'm just curious."

"Well, perhaps what I am about to tell you from the Creator will help you answer questions."

"What do you mean? What will help us?" I barked back at Peter.

"The Creator instructed me to tell you that dogs will be able to enter the gates of Heaven when the Gospel of Sampson is retrieved and fulfilled."

"What's the Gospel of Sampson?" I asked, wondering how difficult it might be to retrieve such a thing.

"Well, frankly, Buster. I'm not sure. The Creator didn't give me any particulars. I did hear rumors of a lost gospel from some of the religious scholars who passed through the gates. They said that in addition to the gospels written by Matthew, Mark, Luke and John, there was a fifth gospel that somehow mysteriously disappeared. The scholars hoped to learn the answers in the heavenly afterlife. But so far they have not."

"Why not?" I asked. "I mean, it sounds like a gospel is a book or manuscript of some kind. If the scholars can't uncover it, what are Bo and I supposed to do? We wouldn't know where to begin such a search. It could be anywhere. Are you telling us, though, that dogs don't get beyond the gates until the dumb book is found?"

"I'm afraid that's exactly the sum of it," replied Peter, who was now showing impatience to return to some more important work than debating the GST with two potential gatecrashers.

"Why did the Creator tell us this information? What are we supposed to do, sit here outside the gates and wait until somebody retrieves the book and brings it to the Creator? We could wait forever," I could feel my voice quivering with stress as I pleaded in vain with Peter.

"My suggestion, Buster, would be that you join Bo and the rest of the dogs in Green Valley. After all, that was the place where the Creator fashioned the first dog. It's supposed to be the ideal place for dogs to run, and jump, and frolic, and laze away in the shady warmth of an oak tree next to a quiet stream. It's dog Heaven. Pure and simple. You can enjoy it forever."

I looked at Peter and scoffed. "It may be dog Heaven, but that means that Heaven isn't really going to be Heaven for Debby. Not unless I'm there. So we better get this Gospel of Sampson book retrieved before she arrives at the gates."

Peter forced a smile as he challenged Bo and me. "Well, then, gentle creatures, it sounds like you've got your work cut out for you, doesn't it? Who knows, maybe the Gospel of Sampson is actually buried in Green Valley?"

"Is that what the Creator said?" I asked Peter as he prepared to leave.

"No, the Creator didn't give any clues. But if you ask me, it would make perfect sense to look there," Peter responded.

"Why?"

"Think about it. It's the one place on Heaven and earth that has never been explored by the humans who have searched for the missing gospel. Doesn't that make it a good bet?"

With that remark Peter disappeared from the gates.

I looked over at Bo. He shrugged his shoulders, and said:

"Beats me what all this missing gospel talk is all about. So what's the big deal? I mean the great Creator of everything designs the GST and can't remember where a certain book is placed! Now if that isn't enough to shake one's confidence in the GST, what is?"

"Easy, Bo. Don't get so excited. Roger taught me to be more philosophical about these kinds of things. I've learned from our moments at the wall that humans have a lot of peculiar customs and beliefs. Some of the beliefs don't seem to make sense. But then sometimes the honest-to-goodness truth of a matter doesn't make sense either. Roger told me that since the beginning of human time, humans have had a peculiar relationship with their Creator. The humans like having a covenant. It's a kind of contract agreement with the Creator. The Creator likes putting clues into the religious scriptures that provide insight into the future. The great religious teachers are called prophets, because they have the ability to understand the clues, which allows them to predict the future."

Bo wasn't too keen on what I was saying. He growled and shook his head, like I wasn't making any sense to him. "Are you telling me that the Creator caused religious books to be written that contained clues about what was going to happen in the future?"

"Right, Bo. You're absolutely right. That's one of the basic human word games played with the Creator. It's like chasing balls. Some people never get tired of chasing predictions about the future."

"Why? Why is it so important to know about the future?" Bo asked innocently.

"That, Bo, is a very profound question."

Bo beamed with pride. A broad head-splitting grin spread across his face. He wasn't used to getting praise for his brilliant philosophical thinking.

I continued. "Humans think that if they can predict the future they can control it. It's that simple. Humans want to be like the Creator and control their own destiny."

"Is it possible for them to actually control the future?" Bo asked as he casually scratched his ear with his left rear leg.

"Roger says he never could. He told me that all you had to do was convince other people to think you can predict the future, and they will give you money and hold you in high esteem. Some people become powerful because other people believe they can predict the future. Sometimes people who predict the future get lucky and some of their predictions come true. Roger says that's how some people make a lot of money on Wall Street."

"So why is it important for us to find this so-called Gospel of Sampson?" Bo asked as we both turned and headed for nearby Green Valley.

"I'm not sure, Bo. But it's clear from what Peter said that the gospel is an important piece in the GST. It must contain some very important clues that are needed by somebody. It sounds like there are clues that will help clear up the misunderstanding as to why dogs are not allowed into human Heaven."

"What are we going to do?" Bo asked, as he edged up against a willow tree and made his mark.

I waited politely for Bo to finish. Then I did likewise, making sure I'd elevated my leg appropriately so my mark would be higher on the tree! Bo knew why. It's the nature of things for dogs to show superiority. I was pleased to feel that things hadn't changed in dog Heaven either. By the time I was done, Bo was already over at a clump of shrubs, repeating the ritual. I caught up with him and continued my comments.

"You asked what are we going to do? I'll tell you what. We're going to find and retrieve that book and take it to the Creator in person."

"Do you think that if we show up with the book of Sampson, Peter will let us go and see the Creator?" asked Bo.

"I'm absolutely convinced. I feel it in my bones."

Bo laughed. "Great. Just great. Need I remind you that you no longer have any real bones? Don't forget where you are and what has happened. Wake up, Buster. We're on our way to the center of Green Valley, also known as 'dog Heaven'."

I smiled as I jogged down the dirt pathway to the emerald green valley that was ahead of us. I noticed that arching overhead was a beautiful and glorious rainbow. It was all very nice, but I didn't feel it was really Heaven, especially if Debby would never be a part of it. And I was sure it wouldn't be human Heaven for Debby if I wasn't with her behind the gates.

I looked at Bo and inquired. "Do you know any dog who has been around long enough that he might help us find the missing gospel?"

Bo frowned as he thought about it. Then an idea occurred to him. He blurted out a suggestion. "I've got the perfect place to start. We'll begin with the Beagle. He's the smartest dog in Green Valley."

"Great, Bo. You lead the way."

While I trotted behind Bo, I became conscious that Mr. Harry Hartman was working feverishly at his computer. His passion for completing his role in the Grand Scheme of Things seemed awesome. I didn't know why images of him were part of my awareness, but I sensed it had to do with the urgency of his work and the urgency of our quest to find the lost gospel of Sampson. Based upon what I'd sensed from Peter's conversation with the Creator, Harry's gift somehow fit into the computer program that was being written to bring the Grand Scheme of Things into its final perfection. I had a sense that if Harry was successful before Bo and I were, we'd never get things straightened out in theGgrand Scheme of Things. Bo and I would forever be separated from our humans.

I could almost hear Harry talking to himself as he worked on the Revelations Project virtual reality program.

"They wanted a creative way to bring the GST to an appropriate conclusion. Boy, wait until they see this formula. The images of this program are awesome. It will make the biblical version of the Apocalypse seem like a fairy tale. I can hardly wait to find out how the Creator likes it. If I get approval to go ahead, it will be possible to implement the ending much sooner than the Creator imagined."

Harry leaned back in his chair and put his hands behind his head. A smile filled his face. "I love it when a plan comes together." Harry felt a sense of pride he'd never experienced in his work in the previous life. His destiny was about to be fulfilled.

"Come on, Bo. How much longer before we get to the Beagle's place? We've got no time to spare."

Bo chuckled. "What do you mean, Buster? Relax. We've got all the time in the world."

"That may be true, Bo. But if the world doesn't have much time left, I don't find your wisdom very comforting. Hurry up."

CHAPTER 8

"**B**o, what makes you think the Beagle is going to be helpful?"

"He's the smartest dog ever to live in Green Valley. I've talked with him on a couple of occasions. Or, should I say, I let him talk to me. He keeps pretty much to himself, most of the time."

"What does he do with his existence here in Green Valley?" I asked.

"He digs up things and studies them."

"Oh, I see. He's a kind of archeologist?"

"What's an arf-e-ologist?" Bo asked as we stood on the hillside overlooking one of the countless dog settlements in Green Valley.

I got a kick out of Bo's mispronunciation. I thought it was a great pun. Like, "What do you call a Beagle who works for an archeologist? An ARF-E-ologist." Bo didn't get it. I explained it to him as best I could. He got the picture, but failed to see the humor.

"Besides being like his former archeologist owner who traveled around the world digging up things, what makes you think the Beagle can help us?"

"You'll find out momentarily. Here we are."

We stopped in front of a very large Victorian-style house. It was surrounded with a white picket fence. A sign on the fence read, "Beware of Humans." "Cute. Really cute," I thought to myself as we opened the gate and headed toward the porch steps. The yard was a mess. What had once been a well-groomed lawn was pitted with mounds of dirt that could have been dug by some giant mole or groundhog. I suspected, though, they were the works of the Beagle that lived inside.

When we got to the top of the porch, it too was cluttered with everything imaginable, from old bones, fragments of old glass bottles, pieces of driftwood, an assortment of strange and colorful rocks, and countless pieces of old furniture and household appliances. There were also an incredible number of old pieces of pottery and ceramics, which had been placed on makeshift shelves and labeled with little pieces of paper describing what they were used for and what time in the history of Green Valley they were used. The Beagle, it seemed, had learned from his former human the habits of digging up stuff and labeling it. If someone wanted to learn about the history of Green Valley, it was evident from what we saw on the porch that the Beagle was the place to start.

Bo rang the bell, which chimed so loud that for a moment it seemed like the whole house was shaking. Bo didn't seem surprised. As we heard the scratching and scurrying of dog steps coming down the entryway hall on the other side of the door, Bo whispered. "Oh, by the way, I forgot to tell you, but the Beagle is almost totally deaf, so you'll have to really speak up."

When the door opened, I expected to see a prime looking Beagle dog. Instead, there appeared one of the oldest, most arthritic, out-of-shape, overweight Beagles imaginable. The only thing that wasn't old looking was the playful twinkle in his eyes.

Bo spoke first. "Zack. You sure look a lot older than you did when they finally put you down!" Bo turned his head slightly and whispered to me. "Zack is unlike the rest of us here in Green Valley. He thinks things that appear to be old are superior to things that are new and fresh. I think that's a value he picked up from Doc Abe, his human archeologist, or whatever he was called."

I nodded my head. If old was superior in Zack's self image, then he undoubtedly thought of himself as superior to everybody and everything in Green Valley. It hurt me to watch him move about in the entryway. My first thought was how on earth could such an old and feeble dog expect to maintain a huge house like the one we were about to enter. Soon I realized he didn't expect to maintain it. That wasn't important to him. It was just a place to keep his stuff. And did he ever have stuff!

"Bo. Bo Diddley. I must say, old chap, it has seemed like eternity since I've seen you. Do come in, good fellow, do come in."

He motioned for us to enter, which we did. Zack didn't waste time with formalities. He turned and headed down the long entryway toward a larger room in the distance. The hallway was cluttered with junk, and there was stuff hanging from the ceiling overhead.

Zack turned his head slightly and spoke to us over his shoulder as we made our way behind him. "I was just about to chew on some Asian rawhide twists Doc and I discovered on our digs in Mexico. They've got a really robust, subtly beefy flavor. Excellent. Aged about three to five years, I would imagine."

When we got to the end of the hallway, we turned right into a huge room that was probably one used by his human as a parlor. At that point Zack turned to examine both of us more carefully. He walked twice around Bo and sniffed and bumped him playfully. I could tell he liked Bo. Then he looked over at me. He took great pains to study me up and down very carefully before he sniffed me once over. When he finished, he was nose to nose with me. I was relieved to see he was smiling, even though it was one of those smiles that says, "I know more about you than you think I know." I soon found out how true this proved to be.

Zack turned to Bo and said, "So this is the Retriever I've heard so much about, the one that created such a stir by barking at the gates. I'm pleased to meet you, Buster, you're exactly as I imagined you would be."

Zack didn't wait for me to respond. Instead, he turned and rummaged through one of the numerous mounds of stuff strewn all over the room. Moments later, he flipped several rawhide twists into the center of the floor and invited Bo and me to join him. We obliged. All three of us settled comfortably onto our bellies in a clear spot in the middle of the room. We chewed our rawhide a few minutes. I looked over and caught Bo's eyes. I was looking for some signal that it was O.K. for me to begin some serious conversation with the Beagle. Bo gave me a frown as he wrinkled his forehead slightly. It wasn't right yet.

Bo had been through this routine before. He knew that Zack would be anxious to talk about one of his many projects. He looked forward to the infrequent visits from both friends and strangers because such occasions provided him a forum to hold forth with his theories and his conclusions.

"What have you been up to since we last spoke?" Bo inquired as he gnawed at his rawhide twist.

"Oh, you know Bo, same old same old," responded Zack as he struggled to raise himself onto his front two legs. A silly little smile turned up one corner of the Beagle's mouth, as though he'd been waiting for someone to give him the lead. He looked over at me to see if I caught the humor of his remark. I smiled. It was self-evident. This dog was into old.

Bo smiled to show appreciation for Zack's wit. Bo seemed to know the next line as well, as he continued the conversation. "So, have you dug up anything interesting lately?"

"Everything I dig up is interesting. Why wouldn't it be interesting?" Zack barked louder than was necessary for our small room and it was difficult not to be annoyed. I did my best not to show it.

Undaunted, Bo continued. "Of course, Zack. What I meant to say was, "What's the most interesting thing you've dug up recently?"" I was really impressed at how patient Bo was with the old Beagle. It was a good thing, too, because I was in no mood to engage in such idle chatter. I wanted to get to the point about the missing Gospel of Sampson. In the back of my mind I could sense that Harry Hartman was working frantically to complete his final piece of the Revelations program.

Zack raised his sagging body onto all four legs and shuffled to another pile of stuff in the far corner of the room. After pawing around for a few moments, he returned carrying an old leather collar. Zack carefully spread it out flat on the floor in front of Bo and me. I was supposed to be impressed, but I didn't have the slightest reason to be; which, of course, was precisely the effect

Zack intended. After Bo and I examined it for a few moments, Zack spoke.

"Quite a find, wouldn't you say?" I looked at Bo. Bo looked at me. I could tell Zack was anxious for one of us to acknowledge our ignorance, so he could display his superior knowledge about such stuff. I finally asked the question Zack was waiting to hear.

"What is it, Zack? It just looks like an old, half-rotten dog collar. What's its significance?"

"Ah, my boy, get close and give it a good sniff. You, of all creatures, should smell something strange about it. Go ahead, give it a real sniff. See if there isn't something in the back of your senses that connects with the collar."

I walked over to the collar and put my nose right down against the leather. Slowly, I moved from one end of the collar to the other. And about halfway through the examination, a strange sensation formed in my mind. I began to feel a connection to the scent. I should have known the scent, but I didn't.

Zack watched intensely as I made my examination. It was as though he were relying on my senses to verify what he already knew to be the importance of his find. When I looked up from the collar, I could tell that Zack was elated. He'd seen the element of surprise on my face as I realized it was a familiar scent. He also knew I couldn't make any meaningful connection.

"So, Buster boy, anything seem familiar about the collar?"

"Well, sir, it does provoke a very distant sense of familiarity. It's like an old scent that reminds you of somebody, but you can't remember who. Am I supposed to know whose collar it was?"

"Not at all, boy, not at all. Do you know what that collar is?"

We both shook our heads, "No."

"Well, let me tell you. It's the very first collar ever worn by a dog here in Green Valley. I'd date it back to the very beginning of time. I'd guess from the markings on the leather that it was worn by the very first dog designed by the Creator. It was obviously made by the first humans who felt the need to have some control over the dog."

Bo and I looked at each other and could not believe the good fortune that had befallen us. Here at the Beagle's place, we were looking at a piece of tangible evidence that connected us to one of the original dogs.

"That's incredible," I said, as I examined the collar again. As I sniffed it carefully, a smile came across my face.

"It's a Golden Retriever. That's it. That's what I smell. My god, I can't believe it. You mean this was worn by my great, great, great, great, etc. grandfather! Incredible. I can't believe it."

Zack raised himself to full stature and puffed out his sagging chest with pride. "That's it, Buster. The one and only. Now isn't that more exciting stuff than some newfangled yuppie leash that self-retracts its own slack! I could get a king's fortune for that little artifact if Doc and I were still digging around before we both arrived here in the afterlife."

"Do you mean your human is over there behind the gates and you're here?"

Zack nodded, and a sad look washed across his face. I could see tears forming in his eyes.

"That's the way of the Grand Scheme of Things. Didn't old Peter make it clear to the two of you when you presented yourselves at the gates? That's the perfect GST." There was a tone of resentment in the old Beagle's voice as he continued.

"I'm convinced, though, that it isn't going to be that way forever. Even a dumb dog knows that Heaven can't be Heaven in the Grand Scheme of Things if it separates dogs from their humans. There is clearly a glitch in the old GST. Change will come to pass. That's why I'm not about to change how I last looked when Doc Abe went to meet his Maker. When it comes to pass that things are corrected in the GST, I don't want old Doc to see me any differently than he did before."

I looked down again at the collar. I again shook my head in disbelief. "So this is the collar that was worn by Sampson, the first dog. The great Golden Retriever. Amazing."

Bo looked over at me. I seemed mesmerized by the collar and what it represented to my personal genealogy as well as the history of all dogs.

"I think it's about time you told Zack why we came, Buster."

"Gosh, Bo, you're right. I almost forgot." I paused again and looked down at the collar. I tried to imagine it hanging around the neck of the very first Retriever, the Retriever that was surely called Sampson.

"Zack, when we were last at the gates, we learned from Saint Peter that the Creator knows I'm related to Sampson. The Creator said that there were certain things written in a lost manuscript called the Gospel of Sampson. Something is written in that Gospel that must come to light and be fulfilled before things will change and come into the final form that the Grand Scheme of Things is supposed to take in the end. Your human is already behind the gates. It won't be long before mine arrives, too. That's why Bo and I need to find the missing Gospel. We've got to straighten out things in the GST. Once we find the book, we'll know what needs to be done. We figured that there's only one place that humans couldn't explore. That's here in Green Valley. This is the place from where the Creator banished humans in the very beginning. So we figured this is where to look. That's why we're here. You've dug around here. So we thought we'd start with you."

Zack's face took on one of those philosophical looks that I was used to seeing on Roger. "Doesn't it seem more than coincidental that I would find the collar and then you would arrive at the gates? Then you come to make your visit? Maybe, just maybe, there is a Grand Scheme of Things that is still unfolding. Maybe we've underestimated the Creator after all. Maybe the Creator has a plan that does finally include both humans and dogs."

I shared Zack's perspective. And my impatience began to show. "So, if you found Sampson's collar, all we have to do is go to the same place and start looking for the manuscript. Where did you find the collar?"

Zack frowned. "Actually, I dug it up at one of the new subdivisions in the hills north of here. You know where I mean, Bo. It's the new settlement that the Terrier is in charge of developing. A lot of the new arrivals are settling there. I was supposed to make sure there were no significant historical artifacts buried there before the Terrier started his subdivision. When I found the collar, I thought the Terrier was going to die all over again. He keeps thinking that's he's back on earth with his human and there's a profit to be made in subdividing the land. He doesn't seem to appreciate that here in Green Valley the land expands to meet the needs of the dog population. But I guess we all have a hard time losing the behaviors of our previous owners. The Terrier had a human named Murray in his life on earth.

I looked in disbelief at Bo. Another coincidence, maybe? Wasn't Murray the name of the escort who brought Harry to the gate?

"So, Zack, what's the problem?"

A frown grew on Zack's face, and he seemed hesitant to tell us about the deal he'd made with the Terrier.

"The Terrier knew the moment I found the collar that I wanted to keep it. He didn't want me to slow down the development by conducting a thorough search of the landscape for artifacts, so he told me I could keep the collar if I'd sign off. I was almost done with the study, and there were only a few more places to look, so I made the deal."

Zack was distressed by the thought that he may have interfered with things happening the way they were supposed to happen in the Grand Scheme of Things. His innocent deal with the Terrier may have resulted in the ultimate destruction of the Gospel of Sampson.

"What are we waiting for? It sounds like we better go and get permission to look around for the missing manuscript," I said as I stood up and headed for the door.

"Not so fast, Buster, boy. I can't go with you. I promised the Terrier I would stay completely away from the property."

"So what are we going to do?" I asked, as I stopped in the doorway to the huge room. The Beagle was rummaging through another pile of stuff, and finally extracted a map of the Terrier's subdivision. He spread it out on the floor and pointed to one plot of land.

"There. That's the one place where I didn't complete my search. It's probably the last place in the subdivision anyone would want to settle. I suggest you and Bo go and see if you can arrange for that place to be where you locate your mansion. Once the Terrier deeds it to you, then you'll be free to dig all over the place. If the missing gospel is there, I'm sure you'll find it."

Both Bo and I examined the map very carefully. We noted all the markings that we could expect to find around the boundaries of the plot. I thanked Zack for his cooperation, for the tasty rawhide, and his great help. As we started to show ourselves out, the Beagle barked at us to stop.

"Here, take this, Buster." He tossed the priceless collar toward us. It landed on the floor right at my feet.

"Wear it when you search, Buster. It may help you match the scent of Sampson with the location of the manuscript."

I hesitated to pick up the collar and take it, knowing how proud the Beagle was of his discovery.

"I really shouldn't take it, Zack. It's yours. You found it."

Zack looked up at us and smiled. "Don't think I'm not being selfish, boys. Wouldn't you give up your most precious thing if you thought it would reunite you with your human in Heaven? Now what are you waiting for. Get on with it."

I picked up the collar and Bo helped me snap it in place around my neck. I was probably imagining things, but it almost made me feel magical as we made our way down the cluttered hallway and out the front door.

I looked over at Bo as we began jogging down the street toward the hillside where the Terrier's new subdivision was located. Bo had a determined Bulldog look on his face. "We're going to find that gospel aren't we, Buster?"

I nodded to show my determination. I was being distracted by my desire to keep in tune with Harry and his work on the Revelations Project. I struggled to focus my awareness on Harry.

"Harry!" Harry recognized the familiar voice that shouted his name from across the street. It was his friend Murray. He hadn't seen him since the trip across the Door of Light and the moment at the gates.

"Murray. It's good to see you. How's business? Still working the real estate angles here? I can't imagine it would be Heaven for you if you couldn't."

Murray looked the same as he did when he escorted Harry to the gates. There was the smile on his face, the gold chain around his neck, and his paunchy stomach that hung inelegantly over his belt. Murray was glad to see Harry. And this time Harry was glad to see somebody familiar. He'd been so engrossed in Project Revelation, it was good to see somebody who didn't fret about such things.

"So, Harry, what's going on. Has the Creator got you working full time on some secret and special project?"

Harry was a bit taken back at Murray's the candor and insight. It surprised him that Murray knew exactly what his friend was doing. He wondered if anything was secret in the heavenly afterlife.

"Well, as a matter of fact, I am working on something that is very exciting."

"Don't tell me. You're working on the Revelations project. Right?"

Harry looked around to see who was observing their conversation. He was so used to industrial espionage in his former life, he couldn't shake the feeling that there might be somebody who was listening who shouldn't be. Murray sensed his uneasiness.

"Harry, when are you going to lighten up? There's nobody here who isn't on our side. It's O.K. I'm on the network. Everybody here is. It's no big deal. I'm just one of the people who happens to be interested in the Revelations Project. Many people aren't. I think it's fantastic that the Creator has enough sense to bring all of that former life stuff to an end. Why should anybody be denied immediate access to this superior form of existence as soon as possible? And why shouldn't the evil forces finally get their eternal due?"

Harry smiled, nervously. He relaxed a bit and began talking about the program he was developing.

"Murray, I've got this wonderful program that is just about complete. I call it the Apocalypse Perception. It's modeled after the scriptures. With what we know about virtual reality, it's really a relatively easy way to create the most terrible and frightening final perceptual experience for those who are aware of the final moments of time. It's going to be awesome."

Murray smiled, thinking about all he knew about the souls that were tortured and subjected to man's inhumanity to man.

"Tell me, Harry, what's going to happen to all of those souls who have been denied entrance to Heaven for the crimes they've committed against other humans?"

"That's the really great part of my program. They'll be fully aware that time is ending and that their souls will be frozen in time. And they will be aware of a fire that will begin burning at the boundaries of their perception, and they'll be aware of and able to perceive their own existence consuming itself. They will be aware of the fact that they are dying forever. I tell you, Murray, it's awesome."

"So when will it be put into place?"

"I'm not sure. As I was programming it into the Grand Scheme of Things, there was a peculiar code that prevented me from executing the implement command. All I could do was write and program the approach plan. Deployment is in the hands of the Creator. I think there are some things that must happen before the final execute command is entered."

"Tell me, Murray, have you ever heard about some person called 'Sampson?'"

Murray frowned and shook his head. "No. Why do you ask?"

"Just curious. I have the feeling that Sampson isn't a person."

"So, who is Sampson?

"I think he's a dog."

"A dog? That's impossible. Look around, there aren't any dogs here. Do you see any dogs?"

"Precisely my point, Murray. Haven't you ever asked yourself why there are no dogs here? Didn't you have a dog in your former life?"

A frown spread across Murray's face. Until that moment, his mind had been unconnected to memories about the loving relationship he'd had with his dog. Tears started forming in his eyes. It surprised him. It was the first time he'd experienced any sadness in the afterlife. This startled both Murray and Harry. They looked around to make sure nobody else had noticed. Murray wiped his eyes.

"My god, Harry. Until you mentioned it, I'd forgotten all about my dog, Tommy. I took him everywhere with me. He knew more about my business than most of my associates. He died several years before I did. I used to joke that if there was real estate deals to be made in dog Heaven, then he'd be the king. Say, didn't you have a dog as well?"

Harry nodded. He felt tears welling up in his own eyes as he recalled how much he loved his German Shepherd, Larry.

"Wow, Murray. Larry was the most loyal, obedient, and compulsive dog I ever owned. I used to wish I could have some of my programmers programmed with Larry's discipline and doggedness. He was wonderful."

"How come we don't get to be with our dogs here in Heaven?" Murray asked. They both shook their heads in bewilderment.

"You know what I think, Murray?"

"What?"

"I think that some dog named Sampson has an important role to play in bringing the Grand Scheme of Things to its complete perfection."

"You'd think if a dog has an important role, the Creator would reward him with a place in Heaven."

"Yeah, but it wouldn't seem fair to have only one dog here. Maybe the Creator will reconsider and let all dogs into the final scheme of things," responded Murray, as he thought about his own dog, Tommy the Terrier.

"Well, something important has to happen with this creature

named Sampson before the Creator will deploy the execute command on the Revelations Project."

"Let's hope for the best, my friend. Let's hope for the best."

CHAPTER 9

We were still a distance away from the Terrier's subdivision when we began to see signs appear alongside the trail. "Tommy Terrier's Exclusive Green Valley Mansion Sites." "Tommy's Dream Sites: Heavenly Views." "The Nearest Thing to Heaven, Just Ahead."

"I have the feeling, Bo, that this Tommy Terrier is quite a character. Is he the dog who brokered your place?"

Bo scoffed. "It really isn't like there's a choice, you know, Buster. The Terrier is in charge of all real estate transactions here in Green Valley. It's what he does best. It makes him feel important to be the land wheeler-and-dealer. He has the gift of making everybody feel like they're getting a good deal. I mean, how can you not have a win-win-situation. All sites require no money down and no monthly payments. All Tommy negotiates are the interest rates. Sometimes he gets as high as 18 or 19 percent on an eternal fixed-rate mortgage. I got a great deal after haggling for what seemed like forever: 6.4%, with no points and no closing costs."

"Wait a minute, Bo. If there is no money down, no points or closing costs, and no monthly payments, what difference does the interest rate make? It doesn't make any sense."

Bo looked at me like I was one of the dumber dogs in Green Valley.

"It doesn't make any difference to me as a buyer, but it seems to be really important to Tommy the broker. But you're right, Buster, it doesn't make any sense. Whoever said selling and buying real estate made any sense anyway? I mean, who on earth ever came up with the idea that anybody could own land? That's what's really absurd."

"So, why is this Tommy Terrier pretending to sell land in Green Valley?" I asked curiously.

"Because it's what he does best," responded Bo, as though his answer should have been self-evident.

"Oh," I said, and then dropped any further discussion about the sensibility of selling something that is in unlimited supply. I was beginning to learn that there are certain traditions that continue long beyond their usefulness. That's what tradition is all about. Buying and selling stuff and ownership seems like it's such a powerful habit that even in Green Valley it is necessary to preserve the tradition.

When we arrived at the entrance to the new subdivision, it was obvious that selling land in Green Valley was quite an event. There appeared to be an endless line of dogs queued up at the entrance. Bo took one look at the line, and said. "Come on, Buster. I've been here once before. There is an easier way. Follow me."

I wasn't sure where Bo was going, but he seemed to know. We ducked under the ropes and headed to the back door of the sales office. Bo bumped once or twice against the door before it opened. There was an attractive young Golden Retriever female that smiled as she saw Bo.

"Well, Mr. Diddley. How may I direct your business?"

"Come on, Suzie, you're not on switchboard duty. My friend here is named Buster Tobias Sampson. He's not used to standing in line. Is there something you can do for me to get him an appointment with Tommy or one of the sales representatives? He's just in from California and he's really beat. You're looking really great, kid. I'll owe you one. And I won't forget. What do you say, Suzie? Be a sport and let us in. How about it?"

I'd never seen this hustler side of Bo Diddley. I had no idea he had such charm with the opposite sex. It was amazing. He really had the gift. The beautiful Golden seemed to melt with his charm.

"Well. Mr. Diddley, I could probably make an exception in your case. Why don't you and Mr. Sampson come this way? I'll put you in sales booth three. It shouldn't be long before Tommy can work with you. Please follow me."

Bo swaggered to the door and winked to signal me to follow. I had no idea what this real estate sales transaction was all about, but I trusted Bo. I felt somewhat like the way I did the day Roger took me with him when we bought the new Buick. But I thought that land in Green Valley was more important than a car. And that was my first mistake.

I followed Bo down the hallway and through the corridor of the sales department. When we arrived in the sales area, the Retriever called Suzie opened the door and escorted us into the cubicle. I saw the sparkle in her eye and made a mental note to find out more about dog social stuff in Green Valley. I was curious whether dogs that were fixed in their previous lives became naturally unfixed in the afterlife. I felt a strange tingling sensation in the presence of Suzie that made me feel that all bets were off as far as sexual neutrality was concerned in the hereafter. But that was a question for later. Now we were here in Tommy Terrier's real estate office, and I was about to negotiate the deal of my afterlife.

Bo and I seated ourselves in one corner of the office. There was a very suggestive picture of a dog on a calendar that didn't have any days or months listed. It simply said, eternity. I looked at the dog and thought to myself that it wouldn't be a bad thing to have such attractive female dogs around me for eternity. But, I also realized that it would be far better to have Debby and Roger nearby, if I had a choice. And if I didn't find the lost Gospel of Sampson, then the best thing I would ever have would be a calendar image of a good-looking Golden Retriever. And if I had a choice, I'd take Debby any day!

In a few moments the door opened and in trotted a cocky little Terrier that I was sure was Tommy. I was right.

"Well, howdy, partners. Mr. Bo Diddley. I haven't seen you in a coon's age. Still chasing that little sheltie down by the old duck pond? You rascal. Just because I sold you the best parcel in this whole subdivision, you think you can take advantage of all the innocent little critters that come here unattached?"

I couldn't help myself as I looked at Bo. I knew my eyes were the size of my favorite dog treats. I was hearing about a side of old Bo I'd never imagined before. When we were on earth, I'd never heard him even whisper about female dogs. In fact, sometimes I thought he was a bit strange, if you know what I mean. He never talked about females. Now here in the last few minutes I find he's a real Romeo. I think Bo was blushing a bit, but I couldn't be sure. Tommy was continuing with his patter.

"So, you convinced your old partner here to set up his digs in the new subdivision. All right, Bo. I know you have good taste. No doubt about it. But what about your friend? How about a formal introduction, Bo? I'm pleased to meet you...your name?"

"Oh, Tommy, let me introduce you to my pal, Buster. Buster, this is Tommy. Tommy Terrier."

"Pleased to meet you, Mr. Terrier," I responded.

"Hey, Buster, just call me Tom. Tom the doggone best land hound!"

"Nice to meet you, Tom," I said as I rubbed my nose carefully against the side of his cheek. For some reason, I didn't feel totally comfortable. But it seemed like the right thing to do. He did the same.

"I know exactly what you want. You want a view lot with plenty of running room. Right?"

"Well, not exactly, sir," I responded. "I really have a specific site in mind. I've been talking with Bo and he showed me a map of your new subdivision. If you can accommodate me, it shouldn't take up much of your time. I know there are a lot of dogs just dying to get into this place."

"Hey, Bo, you didn't tell me your friend has a sense of humor. My godness, it's so rare these days. I like it. Dogs just dying to get into this place. It's not original, but it's still funny."

"Look, Tommy. I do have a particular parcel in mind. It's parcel 123 in the north sector. I've seen the map. It's exactly the place I'd like to call my final resting place."

"Well, let's see what we can do. I always like a client that has a firm notion of what he wants to buy. Let's see what the computer says. Come on into my command center. Let's see what's still available."

Bo and I followed Tommy into a large room adjacent to the dozen or so sales cubicles. It was the place where the closing of deals took place. Tommy walked us over to one of the computer operators and introduced us.

"This here is Larry. He's my main computer man. He rewrote the whole Green Valley real estate program. Anybody who is living here is in his new data base. He's phenomenal. Larry, is plot 123 still available? Mr. Buster Sampson is interested in purchasing it. We haven't talked terms yet, but he's definite. Can we deliver it?"

Larry was a tired-looking German Shepherd. Judging from the neatness of his work area, he had all the organizing and systematic traits of the breed. He was very precise in his response. He didn't even look up from his keyboard as he typed in an inquiry.

"I'm sorry, Tommy. Plot 123 is no longer available. It was recently acquired by a Pitbull. He liked it because it was isolated. I got the sense he was very anti-social. But we do have plot 124. It's right next door. I guess it will depend on whether anybody wants to be a neighbor to an unneighborly Pitbull. We do have several other attractive lots, if Mr. Sampson is interested. But Plot 123 has been sold."

Tommy didn't seem disturbed in the least at the knowledge that the plot I wanted was unavailable.

"Hey, partner, it's no big deal. I'll let you in on a little secret. It doesn't make any difference which parcel you pick. The real kicker is what you put on it. We can give you virtually any size, type, color, style house and view you want. You can look at the Swiss Alps out your kitchen window and the ocean surf out your living room. You can have the Grand Canyon in your front yard if you want. That's the beauty of it here in Green Valley. It can be virtually anything you want."

"But I wanted lot 123. I really did," I insisted, thinking I could work out some kind of trade with someone else. But I knew instinctively that I wouldn't want to try and negotiate a trade with a Pitbull. It didn't seem likely Tommy Terrier was too anxious, either. I soon learned he wasn't.

"Look, Mr. Sampson, I've got a lot of clients waiting out there. I did you a favor. If you're not interested in lot 124, then we're both wasting each other's time." I saw him look impatiently at the door. I wasn't sure what to do next. I decided that proximity would have to be good enough. If I couldn't locate my place on 123, at least I could be close enough to perhaps do some sniffing around in a way that wouldn't bother the Pitbull. It seemed like a workable compromise.

"O.K., Tommy. You've got yourself a deal. I'll take 124. But can I just lease it for awhile? I don't need to build right away."

Tommy let out a loud laugh. "Hey dog, get with the program. Nobody leases in Green Valley. It isn't like you're going anywhere else. If you were destined for The Other Place with all the Black Cats, you'd already be there. When you pass the screening and arrive at Green Valley, you're in for good. We don't do rentals, leases, and resales. What you buy and what you build is what you get! Hey, come to think of it, I like that. It has a ring. Larry, make a note of it. We'll use it in the next phase of our subdivision."

Before I could get another word in, Tommy had me sitting down next to Larry the German Shepherd computer operator. Both Bo and I noticed that there was a strange similarity between Larry and the Harry we'd seen with Murray at the gates. Whoever said humans don't start looking like their dogs? We both noticed that Larry was also pretty adept with computers, a trait that Tommy quickly boasted about.

"You're gonna love this stuff, dogs. It's great. Larry here is the best. I mean the very best. He's really put our new technology on the cutting edge. There's nothing better anywhere. It'll be years before they ever see anything like this on earth. And they may never see it the way our projections show things headed anyway…but that's another story. Show 'em how it works, Larry. It's all yours."

As soon as Tommy stopped talking, Larry lit up with

excitement. In a moment you could see he was the brains of the operation.

"O.K. Mr. Sampson—" I interrupted him and said, "Please call me Buster."

"O.K. Buster, here's where your plot is located in the subdivision. Now, as you can see from the screen, we have a cube that represents the virtual space of your plot. What we have to do now, before Tommy can give you a price quote, is to design what you and anybody occupying consciousness in cube 124 will see and experience."

"How do I do that?" I asked, as I looked at the isometric projection of a cube etched in the glow of Larry's computer screen.

"Face #1 is the front boundary of your cube. It's what you sense and experience when you enter the plot. Face #2 is the west boundary. Face #3 is the north boundary. Face #4 is the east boundary. Face #5 is the skyward boundary. Usually that's determined by whether you like high or low ceilings, vaulted, beams, or open sky panorama."

"So what am I supposed to do?" I'd never thought about the fact that down on earth anybody like Debby or Roger had to ever give a second thought to this stuff. I just imagined that somebody else made such decisions. The house that was built on my hill, above Debby's house on Wixson, seemed to be created without any particular human owner input.

Tommy interjected. "It's really simple, Buster. Assume you want a home just like the one your owner had on earth. Just start by describing each face of the cube in terms of something you liked and are familiar with. In fact, that's the kind of place most of our owners choose. It creates the feeling of being home forever."

"Yeah, but without one important ingredient," I added cynically.

"Meaning?" asked Larry.

"Meaning that it isn't the kind of home I want to be in forever without Debby and Roger."

"Oh, yes. Your humans. Of course, I know what you mean.

My human, Harry's wife, used to say he was just as much a fixture in the front room as the old leather couch. He was always sitting there with his laptop computer, hacking away at something as he and Gladys watched 'Wheel of Fortune' and 'Jeopardy.'"

I could tell from the tone in his voice that Larry missed his human. And of course I knew that all of the dogs in Green Valley probably missed their humans as well. It was sort of absurd that we had all the technology to create virtual replications of our homes on earth, but without the humans. That simply made me more resolved to find the dumb missing Gospel of Sampson and get the whole Grand Scheme of Things straightened out, once and for all...before Debby arrived.

Even though it didn't seem like the correct figure of speech, I knew old Saint Peter was going to have hell to pay, if I didn't get things straight before Debby's arrival.

Tommy was impatient to complete the deal, so he began his pressure tactics. "Look, there are others waiting for you to get your design complete. So, what's it going to be? White picket fence surrounding a three-level Victorian? Ranch style with desert view? or mountain cabin?"

I thought for a moment and then realized there was really no other choice. "Let's make it look exactly like Debby's place on Wixson, in Aptos, California."

No sooner had I described my selection than a three-dimensional picture of the Wixson house appeared on the screen. I was shocked. "How'd you do that so quick?"

Larry looked up at me from the keyboard and smiled. "That's one of my newest program features. Once somebody visualizes an image, my system scans their awareness and consciousness data and feeds it into my program. That is an accurate image of what you'd like your Green Valley mansion to look like, isn't it?"

"Yes. Exactly. But how long will it take you to build it?" I asked.

Tommy answered for the German Shepherd. "It's already

built. In virtual reality. Now, all we need to do is agree upon the price."

"But I thought there was no price?" I responded.

"Ah, yes. You're right, technically. But we do need to negotiate the interest rate. I'm prepared to let you have the place for 8.9% interest. Trust me. That's a great rate. Much better than what I've given others."

This seemed so absurd to me. I couldn't for the life of me figure out why this Terrier was so worked up about an interest rate. But somehow it was important to him.

"Suppose I say your rate is too high? What happens then?" I asked curiously.

The Terrier smiled. "Great. That means we'll have to deal. That's what it's all about—making the deal. Here in Green Valley, we know we've got all the time in the world. No problem. We just keep haggling until we find a number that fits both of our needs. Go ahead, give me another number you like."

I looked at Bo. He shook his entire body and frowned. I could tell he was bored. He whispered to me, "Go ahead, give him a number. Let's get this thing over."

I could see Bo's point, so I grimaced and finally conceded, "O.K. I've reconsidered. 8.9% sounds fair. Where do I sign?"

Tommy jumped to his feet and came over to where Bo and I were sitting. He sniffed us both on either side of our heads. "Congratulations. You've got a deal. You're going to really love this place. Welcome. Now you own lot 124. I'll leave you with Larry here to complete all of the details. He'll record the deed to 124 and give you your virtual PIN number. Welcome to Green Valley. Now if you'll please excuse me, I've got some other deals in progress. Good day."

When Tommy was gone from the room, Larry looked up from his work at the keyboard and smiled at me and Bo. "It says here that you're related to Sampson, the first Golden. Is that true?" Obviously, Larry was looking at some data on an information screen that had nothing to do with the Terrier's real estate data base.

"I guess I am," I replied. "But how did you know that?"

Larry motioned us to view his screen, and as he did so he looked quickly around the room and over at the door, to be sure we were truly alone.

"Once a hacker, always a hacker. I can't help it. It was too easy. All I had to do was tinker a bit and I linked with the computer that is the heart of the Grand Scheme of Things. It's kept in the Creator's place behind the gates."

Bo and I joined the German Shepherd in front of his screen. "Unlike all of the other dogs here in Green Valley, I've got one great perk," Larry went on:

"What's that?"

"I can continue to communicate with my former human, Harry, now that he's in charge of the Grand Scheme of Things computer. We've set up a secret channel. It's not as good as having him here, but it is better than nothing. He tells me that there is a rumor floating around behind the gates that a newcomer is sniffing around in Green Valley looking for some lost book called the Gospel of Sampson. It didn't take a genius to figure out that you're the one. It must be important, whatever it is that you're searching for."

I nodded. "It is. We think it's may contain some information that will cause a change in the GST."

"Like what?" inquired the German Shepherd.

"We think it will enable dogs to be with humans behind the gates."

"Wow! Go find it, Buster. Go fetch. What are you waiting for? Let me know if there is anything I can do to help you."

Bo and I thanked the German Shepherd and headed for the door. "We'll keep your invitation in mind, Larry. See you later."

"Before you go, Buster, there's one thing I think you should know."

"What's that?" I asked.

Larry again looked around the room to make sure nobody else was present. He came close to Bo and me so he could whisper.

"My human, Harry, is working on a program for the Creator

that will allow the Creator to complete the perfection of the Grand Scheme of Things. If you don't find the gospel and clear things up, we may not be a part of the final perfect plan. In plain terms, that means we won't get to live for eternity with our humans. According to Harry, there isn't much time left. So please, hurry up."

CHAPTER 10

"This is a great view," Bo exclaimed, as he looked out over the deck, down onto the Pacific Ocean a quarter of a mile away. "It's just like Debby's old place on Wixson." I didn't disagree with Bo, except that the virtual reality images of Debby's house didn't include images of her and Roger. The only improvement in my dream home was that I could have it shaded by the tall eucalyptuses that had been attacked by the tree killers. I could still have the hillside pathway worn bare from the daily scrambling up the hill to find whatever Debby or Roger threw for me to retrieve. That was the nice part about this Green Valley place. It looked better than the real thing that existed for Debby on Wixson Street.

It was really amazing, how this Green Valley subdivision worked. It was a masterful plan, fully computerized. But interestingly, nobody here seemed to think that computers were at all futuristic. They would laugh and tease newcomers to "get real" with their perspectives. Larry, the German Shepherd who helped me construct my virtual reality home, had explained to Bo and me that, "Computers are just a simple tool that can be used by humans and dogs. They are the Creator's pencil, loaned to others who have far less capacity than the Creator to count and record and manage all of the wonderful stuffness of beingness."

When I heard the Shepherd use that expression, I was shocked. I thought it was one that had been coined by one of my humans, Roger.

"Heavens, no," Larry exclaimed. "It's the way we talk about all the things that were designed and deployed by the Creator.

You were fortunate to have a human who could provide you with such insight while you were still on earth."

I brought my thoughts back to the moment. "Let's sniff this place out, Bo. I thought the Pitbull's lot 123 was right next door. All I see, though, are the familiar surroundings that bordered Debby's house on Wixson. I don't see any Pitbull's place." There was nothing that even gave a hint of where the Pitbull's property was located. Bo and I made sure of that as we methodically marked the borders of my new Green Valley property. When we were done, we returned to the house and spread out the map of the Green Valley subdivision on the living room floor.

"There we are, Bo. Right there. And look, the map shows lot 123 right adjacent to my property. But all I see next door is Bill's house and Sheldon's house. Where's the Pit's property?"

"That's the curious thing about Green Valley, Buster. When I designed my place, I made it just like my memory of Pam and Norm's house and property. When I want to go home, I just enter my PIN code into any of the common terminals, like you did when we left the Green Valley sales office. As soon as my PIN clears, I'm aware of my home surroundings. If I've got another dog with me, they're aware of my personal property as well. When I'm ready to leave my private space, I simply use the home terminal, like the one you have over there, to exit to the common space of Green Valley."

As I listened to Bo describe how virtual reality worked in Green Valley, I puzzled over how we were going to access the Pitbull's property. All my instincts told me that it would take more than simply asking the Pit to invite us over so we could sniff around for the manuscript. But the more I thought about what we needed to do, and how all dogs would benefit, the more it seemed that even the Pit would cooperate if we told him the truth.

"We've got to go and find the Pit and tell him the truth. We'll explain to him that the manuscript is buried on his property, and ask him to cooperate so he can be reunited with his human in Heaven. What do you think, Bo? Is that a plan?"

Bo scratched the side of his head. He wasn't too excited

about it.

"I don't know, Buster. You know how I feel about Pits. Even here in Green Valley most of the other dogs walk a wide path around the Pits. In fact, it's really hard to find them in the commons. They keep pretty much to themselves. They don't even like being around their own kind. They're loners. That way, they aren't tempted to get into fights. One dogfight and you're out of this place for good! Everyone knows that. And for some reason that seems to give Pits an awesome amount of power in this place."

"Maybe they're as afraid as the rest of dogs about getting banished. The only difference is that they've managed to convince the rest of us that they're not," I suggested to Bo.

"Yeah, well, I'm not about to test your theory. This may not be human Heaven, but it's a lot better place than where you go if you get into a fight. I'm sure about that. Why do you think there are no cats here in Green Valley? I'll tell you why. I think it's because they always fight. I'll bet if you ever went to Hell, you'd find it's filled with cats—like the black cat that used to pick on Bosley."

I felt a shudder as Bo talked about Hell being filled with cats. I couldn't imagine a more undesirable place to be than an eternity full of cats. Especially black cats. But at the same time, I thought about what was going to happen to Bosley. He was a good cat, and it didn't seem fair that he wouldn't have any other place to go when he died except to Cat Hell. It occurred to me that maybe if all cats go to something like this dog's paradise called Green Valley, it might seem like Heaven to them.

"Do you think Bosley will go to Hell?"

Bo shook his head. He realized that I was quite fond of Bosley. "Well, of course I don't think that's where Bosley will go. He's different."

"Where will he go, Bo, if it isn't to Hell with the rest of the cats?"

"I don't know, Buster. Gosh, why do you always get so philosophical about stuff? Can't you just stop worrying about how it's supposed to be in the Grand Scheme of Things? Have a little faith that there's something good in store for Bosley. Don't start worrying about it. We've got enough to think about right now, don't we?"

Bo was right. He was always so practical. I was getting a bit off the subject at hand. I just filed away the problem about Bosley's afterlife. In the back of my mind I thought about how great it would be to have Bosley living with Roger and Debby and me in Heaven. I didn't even suggest such a thing to Bo, or he might abandon me as crazy.

"O.K. We need to get on with this book hunt. It isn't like we've got eternity to get this stuff resolved. Debby could be knocking at the gates as we sit here. Any ideas on how we get to meet the Pit next door?"

"Well, as disgusting as the thought is to me, I guess our best bet is to exit this place and do some roaming around the commons. If we ask a few of the dogs, I'm sure we'll find somebody who knows the Pit. Anyone who's been around here a while probably knows who owns lot 123."

"Great! Now show me how to exit this place. I've got to get used to all this computer stuff." I motioned for Bo to follow me over to the computer screen that appeared in the corner of the living room. It was curious how whenever we needed a computer screen and keyboard, one appeared out of nowhere.

Virtually no time seemed to elapse between the moment we put my PIN code into the terminal and the appearance of the commons all around us. For someone who had never experienced such a transformation, it really was breathtaking and incredible. But Bo told me that he was used to it.

As we roamed around among the dogs in the commons, there was a whispering message that seemed to trail behind Bo and me as we asked about the Pitbull who lived on parcel 123. Each time we inquired, there was a suspicious and fearful look on the face of the dogs. Nobody seemed to have any knowledge of the Pit we were looking for. There was a general fear, however, that we were looking for trouble.

" Why?" we were asked time and time again. "Why would

anybody go out of their way to search for a Pit? Leave them to their own space, if you know what's good for you." Then as we left each group of dogs, I noticed they would quickly huddle together and begin whispering. After we'd interrogated several groups of dogs, I finally asked Bo, "What's all the whispering about? Have you noticed it too, Bo, or am I getting a bit paranoid?"

"No. I was going to ask you the same thing. Something's going on here, Buster. I don't think they're telling us something that we need to know. I'll tell you what. Why don't you roam around a bit and give me some time to join in the next pack of dogs up ahead? In that way, it won't appear that we're together. You catch up with us in awhile and ask about the Pit. Then after you leave, I can linger and find out what all the whispering is really about."

"Great plan, Bo. Great. I'll just rest here while you run ahead. I'll see you in awhile. Good luck." I jogged over to a giant shade tree and fell quickly into a dog's deep sleep.

When I awoke, I was anxious to catch up with Bo and the next group of dogs. I hurried along the dirt trail that Bo had taken. I could smell his marks along the way, and it was obvious he was not far ahead. Sure enough, I spotted him resting with a group of dogs. The group included a Terrier, a Poodle, and three Dachshunds.

"Good day, brothers. May I join you?"

I cautiously and deliberately walked around and sniffed each dog to make sure there weren't any fear or fight smells. Everything was cool, so I joined them. I winked at Bo, who was doing a great job of pretending he didn't know me.

I didn't waste any time on small talk. "Say, I'm looking for a friend of mine. A Pitbull who lives on parcel 123 in the new Green Valley subdivision. Do any of you know where I can locate him?"

All of the dogs looked at each other, and as in the past groups, they all shook their heads.

"No."

"Not me."

"I make it a rule to stay clear of Pits. You should do the same."

"Goodness, I wouldn't know where to look. And if I did, I wouldn't go looking for a Pit. Are you crazy?"

After a bit of chatter about how nobody likes Pits, I took my leave and started off down the roadway. I winked again at Bo as I left. He pretended to ignore me. As I departed, I heard the dogs begin whispering. "Great," I thought to myself. "Now Bo and I can get to the bottom of this nonsense."

I could hardly wait until he joined me later at a place far down the roadway. In a few moments he appeared.

"So, what is all the whispering about, Bo?"

Bo circled around under the tree where I was lying until he found the right cool grassy spot. As he settled down facing me, a funny little smile spread across his face. He began to chuckle.

"You're not going to believe this, Buster."

"Believe what?"

"You're not going to believe what they are saying about you. It's the strangest thing I've ever heard."

I was getting impatient with Bo. It was so uncharacteristic of him to beat around the bush on anything. "Cut to the chase, Bo. Spit it out. What's going on? What are they whispering about?"

"They are wondering if you are The One. The Golden One."

I couldn't imagine what Bo was talking about. "What do you mean, The One? What's that all about?"

"Well, Buster, here's the story. There is a tradition in Green Valley, one that I was too new to know. Apparently you were not the first dog to question why dogs couldn't get into Heaven. A lot of dogs before you asked the human at the gate why they couldn't join their humans there. The tradition is that there is a record, a book, or some kind of document lost somewhere here in Green Valley. When the book is discovered and in the possession of the right dog, things will come to pass that will cause a change in the Creator's mind so that the Creator will change the Grand Scheme of Things and allow dogs to be with their humans in Heaven."

"So, why all the whispering? Why didn't they just come out and tell us about the tradition? Then we could have told them we were looking for the manuscript and asked their help."

"It's not that easy. That's the other part of the tradition. Apparently, the tradition says that the first dog to discover the manuscript will be unworthy and unwilling to use the document to help make things right in the Grand Scheme of Things."

I still wasn't fully appreciating what Bo had learned. If these dogs had a tradition about the manuscript, then why wouldn't they be anxious to help us find it?

Bo continued. "The dogs' tradition prophesizes that a Golden Retriever will appear and ask about the whereabouts of a certain Pitbull."

"So?"

"So, they all believe that when a Golden Retriever asks about a Pitbull, it is the signal that a great dog fight between good and evil is about to occur."

I was beginning to see where Bo was going with the story. The reason the dogs were whispering was because I was asking a question that was fulfilling their tradition and the prophecy. In their minds, I was The One, The Golden Retriever. What was frightening them was that I was signaling that a great dog fight was about to occur. And everyone in Green Valley knew that when dogs fight in Green Valley, they are banished. And the prophecy didn't say whether good would win out over evil. There was a chance that if I was The One and I didn't win the fight, then the whole scheme of Green Valley might be disrupted, and nobody knew what kind of chaos might occur. Certainly nobody wanted to take sides in this matter. So it was best that each dog simply keep quiet—that would at least prolong the time of the final confrontation.

"Is there anything else I should know about things, now that everybody's determined that I'm supposed to be The One, to straighten out all this mess?"

"Yes, there is one more thing, Buster. But I almost hesitate to tell you. I don't think you're going to like this part one bit."

"What is it? It can't be all that bad."

"I don't know, Buster. What do you think about this? The Pitbull who owns parcel 123 has already told many dogs in the commons that he found the manuscript. He has no intention of doing anything with it except to keep it buried in a secret place on his property. He also made it clear that nobody should cooperate with any Golden Retriever who starts asking about a Pit. The Pit said that if he finds out somebody has cooperated, he will personally find the dog and start a fight. He knows that when he does, he will be banished to where the cats are. He told everybody that if that happens it will destroy the manuscript forever and there will be no chance of ever changing the Grand Scheme of Things. And, as if to make sure everybody knows he's not bluffing, the Pit said that he would prefer an eternity of kicking cat butts to living with a bunch of wussy dogs in Green Valley."

I took a deep breath. "Wow, Bo. It sounds like we've got ourselves one mean bully. I wonder how it happened that he ever got here in the first place? He doesn't seem like he learned much about unconditional love."

Bo nodded in agreement. "That's precisely the point. He didn't. His human was a cruel person who beat him and taught him that it was good to fight and cripple other creatures. The Pit was bred to fight. He never sat by the fireplace with his human and enjoyed the warmth and coziness of a loving environment. He was chained to a post in the human's back yard, regardless of the weather. Is it any wonder the Pit doesn't want to have things changed in the Grand Scheme of Things? If you were the Pit, even if you knew your human didn't make it to Heaven, would you want to be around humans? Would you trust any humans? Right now, being without the presence of an abusive human must truly seem like Heaven to the Pit."

We both became sad at the thought of a creature who was so unloved that he would knowingly prevent things from becoming right in the Grand Scheme of Things. I thought about how many humans there are who are so hurt and alienated from loving relationships that they do bad things to keep others from enjoying all the wonderful stuffness of beingness.

Bo and I were startled by a deep gruff voice. "Excuse me, Mr. Golden, but I heard you were asking about the Pit. I think I can help you."

It was a miniature Mexican Chihuahua that couldn't have been more than five or six inches tall. Its voice sounded gruff like a Rot's. It was such a contrast that the little creature could see the surprised look on our faces. It was a look he'd seen before.

"I know what you're thinking. I'm so little and my voice is so big. That's what everyone says. I think the Creator gave me such a deep voice so that I'd have courage that is disproportionate to my size. That's probably why I'm not afraid of the Pit's threats. As long as it was dark and nobody could see me, I could bluff the best of them out of fighting with me." The little dog lay down between us. He was so small we were both worried that if we moved too fast we might squash him. But to hear him talk, it sounded like we had a really heavyweight partner on our side.

"What's your name?" Bo asked the little guy.

"Joseph. I was named by my human who was a priest in a village outside of Mexico City. He told me I was named after the husband of Mary, the mother of Jesus. You can call me Jose."

"It nice to meet you, Jose," I said in my softest voice, to show respect for his diminutive size. "Do you know where we can find the Pitbull?"

"Yes, but it's dangerous. He lives right next door to my property. I live at lot 122. He's in 123. We're neighbors."

I had a sinking feeling. It didn't seem like this little guy was going to be of much help.

"Oh, I see. Well, my new home is on parcel 124, which borders on the other side of his property. But with all this virtual reality stuff, all I see are my ideal boundaries. I'm not connected to a view of his property. Are you? Can you see his property from your side of his parcel?"

Jose smiled, and his voice boomed out. "Not exactly. But if you promise not to tell anyone, I'll share with you something I've discovered about all this virtual reality stuff. Promise?"

We both nodded.

Jose stood up and quickly ran up and down several times in the space between Bo's body and mine. After a few quick dashes up and back, Jose stopped and spoke in-between breaths.

"You see, there is a very small space of nothingness that exists between the boundaries of each parcel of virtual reality. Apparently, the computer needs to have separate fields or the whole program would get overloaded with data in a single file."

"So? What are you telling us?" I asked.

Jose became animated as he told his story. Without thinking, he lifted his leg and left a mark about three inches from Bo's nose. Bo was startled and felt challenged. Fortunately, he didn't react.

"Oh, excuse me, Mr. Bo. I got so excited," Jose said scratching the dirt where he'd made his mark. To make things worse, he managed to kick a few pieces of dirt into Bo's eyes. I thought Bo was going to digest the little guy in one gulp. Instead, he glared over at me and swallowed three times very hard. I was proud of Bo's self control. He knew we had bigger problems to tackle.

Jose continued his story. "What I'm telling you, Mr. Golden, is that when I heard the Pit next door had dug up the missing manuscript we'd all heard of in our Green Valley tradition, I wanted to take a look at it myself. So I started sniffing around at the boundaries of my property to see if I could find a way into the Pit's turf."

"Did you?"

"Not at first. But one day I found a fuzzy edge."

"What's that?" I asked. Jose looked at me like I was completely computer illiterate. Which I was.

"Are you serious?"

Bo came to my defense. "Hey, he's new here. Computers aren't his thing. So don't pull his chain. Tell him about fuzzy edges."

"Sorry, Mr. Golden. Sorry. A fuzzy edge occurs when a part of the virtual reality program isn't processing properly. It creates a kind of empty hole in the image that is being projected. What I found was an empty space in the boundary. It looked like the mouth to a cave. So I jumped into the spot of darkness."

"What happened?" Bo asked.

"I found myself inside a black tunnel that seemed to go on forever. As I looked back at the spot where I entered, it was now the reverse of what I'd seen from the outside. There was a stem of light where the fuzzy edge bordered my property. I was relieved to know that I could return to my own property whenever I wanted, if I didn't go so far away from the spot that I could no longer see that halo of light."

"I figured that if there was a fuzzy edge on my property boundary, then it was likely there was one on the Pit's as well. I ran through the tunnel until I finally saw a spot of light ahead on the opposite side of the tunnel from where I entered. Sure enough, when I got there, it was simply a matter of going through the fuzzy edge and onto the Pit's property."

As Jose told his story, I could sense he was really proud of his daring adventure. For a little guy, he had a lot of courage. I wasn't sure whether either Bo or I would be anxious to jump into the darkness of a fuzzy edge.

"When you got onto the Pit's property, what did you find?" I inquired.

"At first, I was amazed. There was no human structure such as a house, like the rectory of my priest human that I'd designed for my property. Instead, there were several caves. It was clear that the Pit lived in one cave, judging from the mess that surrounded the mouth. The thing that was most extraordinary, though, was the cave that was right next to the Pit's dwelling."

Without thinking, Jose again raised his leg to leave his mark. This time it came within an inch of my right leg. I winced. I caught the smile that came across Bo's face, as he enjoyed my efforts to show restraint, which I did. Even when Jose kicked dirt all over my leg!

"It was really strange," Jose went on. "Almost like some evil thing had designed an evil shrine. Instead of being darkly lit, like the entrance to the Pit's living quarters, the second cave emitted a strange glow—like eternal flames were burning inside. I cautiously approached the second cave. Just inside was a gate and a series of bars that were like a jail cell, from top to bottom of the cave's opening. But unlike a jail cell, there was no cell door. It was constructed to keep anything from either entering or exiting the cave, forever."

"Could you see anything in the cave?" Bo asked curiously.

"Yes. Oh yes, Señor Bo. There was an altar like my priest human owner worshipped at daily in our church's sanctuary. On it was a book. It was the missing manuscript you are searching to reclaim."

Bo's and my ears perked up. "How do you know it was the manuscript?" I asked, barely able to contain my excitement. "Maybe it was a Bible or some other book. Maybe you were just imagining something that you remembered from your days with your human?"

Jose stood firmly on all four feet and defiantly stared up into my eyes. He didn't seem to mind that my image towered over his tiny frame.

"Mr. Golden, I am telling you that I saw the manuscript. Look at my size. It was not a problem for me to squeeze between the bars. The hard part was to jump high enough to reach the top of the table where the book was placed. Trust me, Señor, it is the manuscript. It is written in funny symbols that I could not read, but there were two symbols on the cover that I did recognize."

"What were they?"

"One was a sketch of a hand reaching from a cloud and tossing a stick. The other was a drawing of a great Golden Retriever! It's the missing manuscript. I am certain of that, Mr. Buster!"

"So what did you do after you got a glimpse of the book?" Bo asked.

"I heard some noises coming from the mouth of the cave. I was sure the Pit was coming. So I jumped down and ran as fast as I could back to the fuzzy edge in the property. Once I entered the tunnel I didn't stop to see what was happening behind me. When I finally got back to the fuzzy edge on my property boundary, I literally jumped through and almost kissed the ground."

Jose theatrically ended his story by reenacting it for us.

"What do you make of his story, Buster?" Bo asked.

I thought to myself. If what Jose said was true, which I believed it was, then this whole thing was about more than just a Pitbull and a Golden Retriever. Something had caused this particular Pit to be in Green Valley in the first place. Something caused him to find the property where the manuscript was buried. Something caused him to design his virtual reality dwelling so that it was next to a cave that glowed as though it was protected by some evil spell. The Pit was destined to play a role in the Grand Scheme of Things.

I pondered all this for awhile, then I answered Bo. "I think we've found our manuscript. All we have to do is figure out how we're going to get it away from the Pitbull, or whatever evil force designed the cave in the first place. Any ideas?"

CHAPTER 11

All the while Bo and I were busily planning how to get into the Pit's property and retrieve the manuscript, I was aware of what was happening on Wixson Street. Barely a day passed that Roger and Debby didn't remember something about how important I was in their lives. After awhile, Debby got beyond the teary stage when she cried whenever the name Buster was mentioned. But she was still actively grieving. My leashes were still hanging on the hooks right next to the garage entrance to the house. The half-dozen plastic tennis ball containers still sat on the shelf. My water pan and empty food dish were still on the floor of the kitchen, right next to Bosley's. The toughest times for Debby were always the first thing in the morning and the first moments when she returned from work in the evenings. Sometimes she awoke in the middle of the night from a bad dream. Roger always held her and comforted her.

Roger did not share with her the strange dreams that frequently came to him. Roger truly believed he was in communication with me. I was surprised, too, at how receptive he was when I appeared in his dreams. I knew I was getting through to him. Although he never spoke about the dreams, the most recent one really puzzled him. Roger recorded it in the journal he kept. He knew someday when we were together we could talk about what happened to me in Green Valley. Roger was very aware of how things were not yet right in the Grand Scheme of Things. I was glad that he chose not to tell Debby about what I was doing. I think it would have made things more difficult for her.

One Saturday morning, though, Roger did try to tell Debby

about my journey to the gate. He was sitting at the kitchen table sipping a cup of coffee and reading the newspaper. There was an article in the newspaper about a new movie called "Fluke." It was about a human who died and came back as a dog. As Roger read the movie review, he couldn't help thinking about all the dreams he'd been having about me in the afterlife. He looked over at Debby, who was standing at the sink rinsing breakfast dishes and loading the dishwasher.

"Deb, listen to this." He read the movie review to her.

"Maybe we ought to see the movie," Debby said. "I don't think the plot is as far-fetched as people might think. I think animals and humans can communicate and that they can be possessed with different spirits."

Roger hesitated, then blurted out, "I think Buster communicates with me in my dreams."

"What do you mean, dreams about Buster? What kind of dreams?" Debby asked, returning to loading the dishwasher.

"Well, it's kind of hard to explain. I keep dreaming that Buster is on some kind of quest. He arrived at the gates of Heaven. I know he did because I dreamed about it. But they didn't let him inside. Instead, he went to a place called Green Valley."

Debby turned around and looked squarely into Roger's eyes. She didn't seem to take too kindly to Roger's comments.

"Look, Roger. I'm just beginning to get over the loss of Buster. I know what you're trying to do, but you don't have to create fanciful stories. Buster's gone. I don't need to have you creating fantasy stories to make me feel good."

Roger could see that Debby didn't believe what he was saying. He wasn't making up a story. What he was dreaming was real.

"Look, Deb. I'm serious. Do you want to hear what I dreamed? I really think Buster's figured out how to keep me aware of his presence."

Debby turned away so Roger wouldn't see the tears forming in her eyes. She knew Roger really felt he was still in contact with Buster. All Debby felt was emptiness. She never had any dreams in which she communicated with me.

Roger didn't notice how he'd upset Debby. He blithely began his recollection of his most recent Buster dream.

"I know it sounds silly, Deb, but Buster and Bo are convinced that there is something wrong with the Grand Scheme of Things. To prove their point, they are searching for a lost manuscript that proves dogs and humans are supposed to be together in Heaven. What I dreamed was that Buster and Bo are just about to get in a fight with a Pitbull who has the lost manuscript. If they're successful, then the Creator will have to change the grand scheme. I can feel that Buster is really anxious to get on with the fight. But he's also frightened and concerned that he may not be able to get the book. He knows that so much depends upon his success. All of the dogs in Green Valley are counting on him. And he knows that he's got to get the Grand Scheme of Things straightened out before you and I get to the gates."

Debby listened carefully. She wiped her eyes with the sleeve of her blouse and turned around. A smile spread across her face. She knew Roger really believed that I was still doing something to show my unconditional love for my humans. It was a nice story, Debby thought to herself, even if it was just a figment of Roger's very fertile imagination.

"Oh, Roger. Where do you come up with such ideas? Maybe you should write a new book about Buster at the gates? It sounds like it would be a great adventure!"

"Maybe I will, Debby. Maybe I will," replied Roger with a silly smile on his face. He walked over to Debby and gave her a big hug.

I always felt good when I sensed that Roger and Debby were doing fine. It made me feel good to know that Debby missed me. It also made me feel good that Roger believed that what I was communicating to him through his dreams was true.

But it was time to let my contact with Wixson fade and to focus on the task that Bo and I had before us. We'd decided that if we were going to find a way into the Pitbull's virtual reality, we'd probably need the assistance of a computer expert.

"Come on Buster and Jose, I'm sure Larry will help us," Bo said, as the three of us jogged toward the sales office. Bo was certain we'd find Larry at his computer screen, especially since we knew that was how he stayed connected to his human, Harry, who worked in the Creator's computer center.

When we arrived at the sales office, Larry was busily typing messages into the screen. He was obviously communicating with his human. He seemed startled to see us at the door. He quickly signed off whatever he was communicating.

"Gentlemen, what brings you back? Is there something wrong with your property or the virtual reality design of your home?"

"Relax, Larry. We're friends. I'm sorry we made you cut off your communication with Harry," Bo said.

Larry was startled. "What do you mean, communicating with my human?"

"Come on, Larry. We know what you were doing. There's nothing wrong with wanting to be with your human. That's what we're trying to work out for all the dogs. And that's why we're here," said Bo.

Larry looked at Bo and me and our little friend Jose. We must have seemed like an unlikely trio. But he could tell we were serious.

"What do you know about fuzzy edges?" I asked the Shepherd, as he stirred nervously and continued to fidget with his computer keyboard.

"You're not a very good software designer if your programs develop fuzzy edges, especially programs that create virtual reality. Why do you ask?"

I looked around the room to make certain nobody could overhear what we were about to propose to the Shepherd.

"Have you ever experienced fuzzy edges in any of your programs?" The Shepherd seemed offended at the suggestion that something he created did not reflect his Germanic compulsion for perfection.

"Never!" he snapped.

"I thought you designed the program for this subdivision, Mr. Shepherd?" boomed little Jose's voice. The startled Shepherd looked around to make sure the deep gruff voice actually came from diminutive Jose.

"I beg your pardon, whatever your name is, little guy. I did design this subdivision. It's my program, totally."

"Well then, you better check your program notes, because I live on parcel 122 and I found a fuzzy edge hole in my property line and one in parcel 123. I entered and exited both parcels through the fuzzy edge."

The Shepherd smiled and shook his head affirmatively. Then he cautioned Jose. "You were doggone lucky, little guy. That's all I can say. You were lucky."

"What do you mean, lucky?" I asked. I thought you said there were no fuzzy edges in your programs?" The Shepherd stood up and walked over to a shelf of program manuals that were lined up in orderly fashion in a corner of his office. He pulled down one and opened it, pawing through the pages until he came to one particular passage. Then he read part of it aloud to us, as though we would appreciate all the work he did to document his virtual reality program.

"Fuzzy edges. VRSP 3.4. VR stands for Virtual Reality Subdivision Program. 3.4 indicates that this is the fourth adjustment to the third revised version of the program. It's the state of the art program. Notice whose name is on this manual." The Shepherd showed us the front cover so there would be no doubt it bore his name. He continued with his reading.

"This program is designed to deal with the natural tendency of virtual reality boundaries to develop fuzzy edges. Fuzzy edges occur when programming commands follow alternative pathways in the virtual reality image field. The effect is to expose the program's surface to the natural emptiness that exists in the interstitial space between image planes." The Shepherd smiled as he savored each word he'd written in the manual. He made it sound so simple, but I didn't have the slightest idea what it all meant, except that he was aware of this thing called a fuzzy edge.

"VRSP 3.4 has imbedded in its master file a boundary maintenance process command. At random intervals, the image boundaries are scanned for naturally occurring fuzzy edges. Repair commands are automatic." The Shepherd paused and looked up from his reading long enough to make eye contact with each of us, to make sure we were attentive to what he was about to read.

"And...any conscious matter that may have leaked into the void between parcel boundaries will be disassembled," he again glanced a meaningful look at us, "so that there is less chance of future variation in the virtual reality image field." The Shepherd closed the manual with a loud pop, to accent the finality of his remarks.

"So, you see, little fella, that's why I said you were lucky. My program automatically fixes fuzzy edges and eliminates conscious matter that might accidentally slip into the interstitial void between the surface boundaries. It's a good thing you're so small. The first maintenance scan prioritizes and identifies and fixes fuzzy edges in the whole subdivision in order of size. There are more than twenty-three million surfaces in this subdivision alone. The maintenance scan is programmed to fix the largest first."

Jose was fortunate to get in and out of the interstitial void before it was repaired by the maintenance program. But if a program could be written to fix fuzzy edges, it seemed logical that a program could be written to modify a certain boundary so that one could enter and exit adjacent parcels just like Jose did by accident.

"Look, Larry," I said, "We need your help. Have you ever heard of the lost manuscript? It's called the Gospel of Sampson."

The Shepherd nodded. "Who hasn't? A dog doesn't have to be in Green Valley very long before he hears talk of such things. Sure. I've heard the story. I think it's what every dog wishes were true, because then we wouldn't be isolated from our humans who are behind the great gates. I'm not sure it's much more than wishful thinking. But at least it gives all of us hope."

"Well I'm here to tell you the manuscript exists. Jose here saw it when he took his dangerous little excursion into lot 123, the Pit's place." The Shepherd's eyes grew wide as he listened.

"Now if the property boundary has a program that constantly repairs and prevents fuzzy edges, isn't it possible to create edges in both adjacent planes large enough for Bo and me to get through so we can sneak over and steal back the manuscript?" The Shepherd appeared intrigued by the idea, and he thought several moments before he answered my question.

"Well, you raise an interesting point, Golden. I've never thought about purposefully creating fuzzy edges. But now that you mention it, I suppose I could tamper with the design. But there are risks, serious risks I should tell you about first."

Bo's ears perked up at the mention of risks. "What kind of risks? I mean, it isn't like we aren't already dead. What else could happen?" The Shepherd returned to his keyboard and asked us to stand behind him as he retrieved some information on his computer screen.

"What you see here is the master program. Here's the boundary line between parcel 122 and parcel 123 and parcel 124. Now what I could do is create a huge fuzzy edge in parcel 124 so Bo and you could enter. That would be no problem. Then, I could create a smaller fuzzy edge on the boundary between parcel 123 and 122. In that way you could exit onto Jose's parcel."

"So what's the risk?" Bo persisted.

"Timing. Timing is everything. As soon as the maintenance program detects the fuzzy edge between Buster's parcel and the Pit's it will begin repair. I can make it large enough to create some delay. But as soon as it's done, it will detect the smaller fuzzy edge between Jose's parcel and the Pit's and begin repairs. I can create some diversion by generating fuzzy edges in other sectors of the subdivision, but I've got to be careful I don't create too many or the whole program will crash."

Bo looked at me and I could tell he still didn't know what we were risking. I wasn't sure I did either.

"So, how much time do we have to get in and get out?" I asked.

"Well, as you know, time is only relative to the virtual reality program and how it functions. Otherwise, there is no such thing as time in the Grand Scheme of Things. But time is very real in computer activity. We're just unaware of it functioning when we experience the images created in virtual reality. Computer time is like the water and we're the fish."

"O.K., Shepherd," I said, "all of this is getting too complex for us to really appreciate. How much of this unreal real computer time do we have and what happens if we get stuck in the Pit's property and can't get back?" The Shepherd flashed a sickly smile. I could tell he was frustrated that we were missing the point he thought he was making so obvious.

"Depending on the size of the fuzzy edges I create, I estimate I can give you about fifteen minutes to get in and get out. You've got to enter through 124 and exit into 122. If you happen to get caught in the interstitial space, I can't help you. The master file is outside of my control. Your consciousness will be disassembled and you'll cease to have any awareness of anything. It's worse than being dead. Now we have awareness and perception. The repair command is designed to keep consciousness from forming and eroding the clean boundaries of the virtual reality planes."

"What happens if we just get into the Pit's space and the fuzzy edge on Jose's parcel is repaired?"

The Shepherd frowned. "That may be the worst fate of all. When you enter a virtual reality field without an access number, you're just like noise in that field."

"What do you mean, Mr. Shepherd? I entered without an access number. What's wrong with being what you call noise?" asked Jose.

"When you entered, little fella, the Pit was not aware of your entry. If he'd discovered you, all he'd have to do is enter a Purge command into one of his terminals and your awareness and consciousness would be erased." There was silence in the room. None of us liked the prospect that the Pit could simply erase us. That was worse than a good dog fight.

"There is one other possibility, though. And knowing what I

know about Pits, I'd say it's more than a possibility."

"What's that?"

"There's the possibility the Pit would just not let you ever exit from his parcel. He could enjoy chewing on you forever. You'd become one of his toys. Remember, once you make an unauthorized entrance, you stay forever unless you're purged."

"Now that's what I call being between a rock and a hard place, for sure," commented Bo, as he contemplated his fate should the adventure fail.

I tried to be more upbeat. I was also anxious to get on with the plan. I turned to the Shepherd. "How long will it take you to program the fuzzy edges?"

"I can do it right now. When do you want to start?"

"Give us about twenty minutes of computer time to get back to my parcel. We'll be standing on the boundary and waiting for the fuzzy edge to appear. Give us as much time as you can, but don't risk crashing the system." The Shepherd started the clock on the upper right of his computer screen and began furiously typing commands into his system. He barked over his shoulder as we left the room. "Good luck, Golden. We're all counting on you!"

We must have looked like an anxious little expedition party as Bo, Jose and I stood on the western border of my parcel gazing out at the magnificent view from the deck of my house. We kept looking for something to appear on the surface of the image that would tell us the Shepherd had been successful in creating a fuzzy edge. Jose was the first to spot it.

"Look. Mr. Golden. Over there! See what's happening. That's what it's like. Come on, follow me!" Jose's bravery was as big as his booming voice. By the time Bo and I caught up with Jose he was already through the hole. We had to wait because we needed a far larger opening than Jose. As Bo and I sat looking at the black hole form in the beautiful view from my parcel, it was as though we were watching some unknown force burn a hole into the surface of a postcard picture of the California coastline.

We were both very conscious of time. As soon as the hole was almost big enough we began squeezing through. Bo went first and I followed. It was like crawling out of a hole under a fence into freedom. Only in this case, we were not escaping into any freedom. There was a good chance that we'd be trapped forever, or totally eradicated from consciousness. Then it wouldn't matter if Debby and Roger came to the gates. I would be gone.

Once we found ourselves in the tunnel of emptiness, what the Shepherd called the interstitial void, we could see light at the end. We scurried for what seemed like miles to the fuzzy edge the Shepherd had created in the Pit's boundary. We dove into it as though we were fearful that the eradication program was only inches behind us. I thought I heard a whooshing sound fill the tunnel the moment we jumped clear into the Pit's parcel. It might have been my imagination.

Bo looked up at me as we stood in the Pit's parcel. "Did you hear that?"

"What?"

"That sound in the tunnel?"

"No. I didn't hear anything. It's probably just your imagination. Come on, let's find the cave and get the manuscript and get out of here." I lied about the sound because I didn't want to frighten Bo any more than necessary. But it made me realize that the Shepherd wasn't kidding about the maintenance program. A few more moments and we'd have been cosmic nothingness.

When we caught up with Jose, he was standing on a little rise that looked down on the Pit's cave. Jose pointed and whispered.

"There are the caves. See how the light glows around the entrance to the second cave? The Pit lives in the first. Let's hope he's sleeping."

Bo looked at the cave. "How do you propose we get the manuscript, Buster? I don't think we can just walk in and take it."

Jose had already been thinking about how to get it. He'd been there once before, so we listened intently as he whispered to us.

"Look. I can squeeze between the bars and get the manuscript. Once I get it, I'll drag it over to the bars and push it through to you, Mr. Golden. Then you run like the wind to my side of the parcel and hope that Mr. Shepherd's fuzzy edge appears in time."

"What happens if the Pit appears?" Bo asked.

I could hardly believe what came from my mouth, as I heard myself say, "I'll take care of the Pit. It's the way it's supposed to be in the Grand Scheme of Things."

It all sounded correct. But I knew that I wasn't a fighter. I'd never had a fight with any dog. Oh, well, maybe a barking contest or a snap or snarl or two to bluff off an aggressor. But I was a loving dog, not a fighter. I winced at the thought of having any fight with the Pit. And I also shuddered at the thought of having to be banished from Green Valley for fighting. But if it was necessary to make right the Grand Scheme of Things, I was game.

Soon the three of us were huddled right outside the mouth of the second cave. The manuscript was sitting behind bars atop a table that did look somewhat like a church altar. We had all gagged on the thick smell of evil as we approached the cave. Jose was right. The Pit didn't create this cave. Something far more evil was keeping the knowledge of the Grand Scheme of Things away from those who could make it right.

Jose whispered, "O.K. I'm going in. It shouldn't take long. Keep an eye out for the Pit. Wish me luck!" He scampered into the cave and through the bars without even brushing against one, then made a running leap and landed triumphantly on the table where the book lay.

Bo and I watched from our crouched position at the front of the cave. Then we realized how small Jose really was. The book was as big as he was. But that didn't deter his spirit. He put his head against one side of the book and pushed it carefully to the edge of the table. Then he looked up at us as if to say that he didn't have any choice but to let it fall. We could tell he was concerned that the noise when it hit the ground would awaken the Pit. We held our breath as the book fell. It seemed like it took an eternity before it hit the ground with a dull thud.

Almost immediately, Bo and I heard some growling and stirring from the Pit's cave. Jose was struggling to push the book across the floor of the cave and up to the bars. He was unaware that the noise had awakened the Pit.

"What's going on here?" growled the Pit as he emerged from the entrance of his cave. Bo quickly dashed into the second cave so he could receive the book when Jose pushed it to the bars.

I stood up and took the fierce Pitbull head on. I could feel my legs trembling. I knew I was about to have the fight of my life. The Pit snarled. "So. You've come at last. You're the Golden One I've heard about all this time. Now that you've met your Maker, it's about time for you to meet your destroyer." The Pit growled and pawed at the ground like he was a raging bull zeroing in on a delicate matador. I remembered that Roger once said to me, "Avoid fighting at all costs. But if you have to fight as a last resort, fight as though your life or those you love depend on your victory."

I looked at the Pit and at once felt terribly sad. Just as he was about to charge at me I said, "What's your name?"

He could hardly believe I was asking him his name at the precise time he was about to tear out my jugular vein. He stopped short with his charge.

"What kind of question is that? Don't you understand I'm going to tear you apart piece by pretty little Golden Retriever piece? Why do you care what my name is? Everybody just calls me the Pit."

"Well, my name's Buster. Buster Tobias Sampson the Third." I hoped he couldn't see the sweat forming on my forehead. I was trying to buy time so I could be sure that the manuscript was securely in Bo's mouth. I was confident that Bo could get free while the Pit was occupied with tearing me apart.. The Pit hesitated again. "Freddie. My name's Freddie." As he uttered the name I could tell that it had been some time since he'd ever thought about himself as anything other than the Pit. But some human had given him that name many years ago, and when the Pit uttered it, I knew it caused him to think about his human.

"I'm pleased to meet you, Freddie. That's a nice name. Were you named after someone your human knew?" The Pit snarled. "Yeah, my human said he named me after Freddie Kruger, the killer in 'Nightmare On Elm Street.' Ever see the movie?"

"Wow, your human had a real sense of humor," I joked. Out of the corner of my eye I caught a glimpse of Bo crawling out of the cave with the book in his mouth. Jose was right behind him.

"My human was a cruel man. And he was sick. He didn't love me. And I hate him. You don't have to pretend with me. I know why you want that book over there in the cave. You want to make things right in the Grand Scheme of Things. You think it will be really dog Heaven if dogs can be with humans in the hereafter. Well, I'm here to tell you that I don't want to be with humans. That's why I was selected to guard that stupid cave in the first place. The evil one knew a motivated watchdog when he saw one. So let's quit this jawing, and get on with this fight. I know I'm supposed to end your quest once and for all. You're the one who has to be beaten. And fighting's my game. So forget about my name. I can take you and the blame."

With that the Pit attacked. He was snarling and biting and scratching and growling, a ball of fury. I braced myself as he charged. He hit the side of my body with such force we both fell to the ground. Baring my teeth or any of the bluffing tactics or reasoning I'd used before to avoid fights was useless now. This was the real thing. And the Pit was playing for keeps. He sank his teeth into the softness of my belly, then quickly released, as though he knew it wasn't a vital spot, and went for my front legs. I bit his ear, and he smiled, as though he enjoyed the pain. I tore off a piece of the ear, but it didn't faze him. He retaliated and bit a chunk from my left ear as well, spitting it on the ground, defiantly.

Somehow I managed to get his right leg in my mouth and I began chewing on it like it was an old soup bone. I could taste his blood; it made me sick to my stomach. I heard him groan with pain, but he continued with his attack, still searching for my vital spot, the one he had learned would end fights quickly once it was found. I butted his head with my forehead, but it hurt me more than him. I tried to maneuver so I was on top of his back, where I knew I was safest.

But the Pit was a skilled warrior. He was built low to the

ground and it was difficult to get any leverage on him. When I was standing upright, it was easy for him to get under me and leverage me to the ground. I struggled with all my might, yet he finally maneuvered me onto my back, and I could see the gleam in his eye as he thrust his head forward and found the strong muscles of my neck and throat. He had found his mark, and sank his teeth in deeply. I gasped. The fight was just about over. A Golden is no match for a Pit. That's the way things are in the Grand Scheme of Things. With all the force his chunky body could exert, he flipped my body on its side. He was holding me firmly against the ground in what was surely his death grip. He was snarling with delight, knowing that victory was only minutes away. I was helpless. Then it happened.

My tear-filled and frightened eyes were staring into his bloodshot mean eyes. I saw the delight he felt as he hurt one of his fellow creatures. But as quickly as confidence had come into his eyes as he seized my neck, now his eyes filled with tears and flashed with pain. He released me immediately and began to twist and writhe in pain on the ground. I was stunned. I hadn't done anything. He'd won the fight and it was all but over. Now he was crying and howling for mercy.

"Stop! Stop! Please! No more! No more!"

I stood up and shook myself all over. It cleared my head just enough so I could see what was happening.. There was Jose, hanging from the tail end of the Pit. He had come to my rescue and was now holding the Pit by the most delicate and sensitive part of his anatomy. And Jose was so small that he was simply swinging from the underbelly of the now not so powerful Pitbull.

"Run, Mr. Buster. Run! Bo has the book. I'll catch up with you," boomed the voice of the little warrior, between bites at the private parts of the Pit.

It didn't take me a second to get going. I was in a full gallop as I closed the distance between Bo and myself. He held the book tightly in his mouth as we both looked frantically for the fuzzy edge that was supposed to be in Jose's side of the Pit's parcel plane.

I saw it first and motioned with my head for Bo to follow. When we arrived at the hole, it was obvious that the maintenance program was already engaged. The hole was being woven shut pixel by pixel. Bo jumped through and I quickly followed. Once inside the tunnel we headed for the light coming from an opening in Jose's boundary. It was rapidly shrinking in size. By the time we arrived, we both had to struggle to squeeze through.

On the other side, we sat on the ground and watched the fuzzy edge grow smaller and smaller. Bo looked at me and said sadly, "It looks like the little guy isn't going to make it."

Tears came to my eyes as I realized that Bo was right. "He's the bravest little dog I've ever met. He saved my life and helped us get the manuscript."

Just then, Jose's head popped through the darkness of the small spot that remained in the fuzzy edge.

"Hey, Buster! Stop crying and give me a hand." Bo and I were ecstatic as we scrambled to pull the little critter safely through the hole. Moments after he was through the fuzzy edge was completely repaired and the image of the boundary of Jose's property was properly restored.

Jose was all excited. "Hey, Mr. Buster, we'd make a good tag team, no? Like my priest used to watch on television. We'd be good with Pits. You bait 'em and I bite 'em. We did good, no?" Jose paraded defiantly, high stepping as he marched over to the book and jumped atop it.

"Maybe we should rename this 'Sampson and Jose,'" he said, and we all laughed as Jose sat proudly atop the leather-bound manuscript.

CHAPTER 12

It didn't take long for us to begin paging through the ancient leather-bound manuscript that lay on the ground before us. The cover was embossed pictures like the kind carved in the wall of an ancient cave-dwelling. One icon depicted a large dog chasing a stick that was thrown by a hand protruding from a cloud. Another was a drawing of a Golden Retriever!

I carefully opened the book and noticed immediately how well preserved it was, all things considered. The text was written in hieroglyphics. All we could do was puzzle over the strange symbols that dotted each yellowed page of the manuscript.

"I've never seen anything like them. How are we going to find out what they mean?" I asked Bo.

"Whoever wrote them must have also designed your collar, Mr. Buster. Look. The symbols are very similar," Jose pointed out.

Bo examined my collar and agreed.

"Well, then what are we waiting for? If anybody can understand the symbols it will be Zack. Why don't we take it to him? If he can't, I'll bet he'll know who can," suggested Bo.

Of course Bo was right. I snatched up the manuscript in my mouth and we all began running toward the Beagle's house, like we were being chased by the evil one himself. I didn't break stride once, but did glance over my shoulder to see if Bo and Jose were still behind me.

I dashed up the Beagle's porch steps in what seemed like a single bound. Zack was waiting at the door, almost as though he expected us to arrive just then. He knew we didn't have much time.

"So, is this the missing manuscript? Well, I'll be. You rascals did find it after all. Well come on in and let's have a look."

Within moments we were all huddled over the book as the Beagle scanned the ancient markings. Bo and I knew how to read human writing in the English language, which was nothing like this, but the Beagle seemed to have no problem reading.

"What does it say, Beagle? What is all this mystery we almost saw destroyed right in our presence?" I asked.

"Very interesting, indeed," muttered the Beagle. "It appears to be very similar to some of the early parts of the book humans call the Bible. It's an account of the creation and…well, why don't I just read it to you from the beginning."

THE GOSPEL OF SAMPSON

Chapter 1

1. In the beginning, God created the event which unfolded the cosmos. Then the Creator focused on the heavens and the earth, and began unfolding the Grand Scheme of Things.

2. The earth was without form, and void; and darkness was on the face of the deep. And the spirit of God the Creator was hovering over the face of the waters.

3. Then the Creator said "Let there be light;" and there was light.

4. The Creator called light "Day," and the darkness was called "Night." So the evening and the morning were the first day.

5. Then the Creator said, "Let there be matter in the midst of the waters, and let it divide the waters from the waters."

6. Thus the Creator made the matter, and divided the waters which were under the matter from the waters; and it was so.

7. And the Creator called the matter that was apart from the earth "Heaven." So the evening and the morning were the second day.

8. Then the Creator said, "Let the waters under the Heavens be gathered together into one place, and let the dry land appear," and it was so.

9. And God called the dry land earth, and the gathering together of the waters the Creator called seas.

10. Then the Creator said, "Let the earth bring forth grass, the herb that yields seed, and the fruit tree that yields fruit according to its kind, whose seed is in itself, on the earth," and it was so.

11. So the evening and the morning were the third day.

12. Then the Creator said, "Let there be lights in the cosmos of the heavens to divide the day from the night, and let them be for signs and seasons, and for days and years.

13. Then the Creator made two great lights; the greater light to rule the day, and the lesser light to rule night. The Creator also made the stars.

14. So the evening and the morning were the fourth day.

15. Then the Creator said, "Let the waters abound with an abundance of living creatures, and let birds fly above the earth across the face of the firmaments of the heavens."

16. Then the Creator created great sea creatures and every living thing that moves, with which the waters abound. So the evening and the morning were the fifth day in the moment the Creator designed the Grand Scheme of Things.

17. Then the Creator decided that it would be really neat to have a creature that was capable of giving unconditional love. The Creator said, "Let the earth bring forth the Golden Retriever, and all other living creatures according to its kind; cattle and creeping things and beasts of the earth, each according to its kind; and it was so.

18. Once the Golden Retriever came to life, the Creator saw what He had made was indeed very good. So the evening and the morning were the sixth day. The sixth day was the longest day, because the Creator and the Golden Retriever enjoyed the endless pleasure of each other's company.

19. At the end of the sixth day, the Creator looked around at all of the other dogs and creatures of the earth, and realized that they were sad. They did not have a personal, loving relationship with anything that resembled the Creator.

20. So on the evening of the sixth day, the Creator decided as an afterthought to develop one more species. The Creator said: "This is not the way I want it in the Grand Scheme of Things; all dogs should have a flesh and blood partner. Therefore, let us make a human in My image, according to My likeness. These humans shall have dominion over the dogs, and over all the earth and over every thing that creeps on the earth.

21. So the Creator made humans in the Creator's own image; the Creator made male and female humans.

22. The Creator then blessed humans, and said to them, "Be fruitful and multiply. Fill the earth and steward it; have stewardship over the fish of the sea, over the birds of the air, and over every living thing that moves on the earth. And most of all, give care and love to your dog."

23. Then, after all was done, the Creator blessed the seventh day and sanctified it, because it symbolized the truth that all had been done in six days. This was the day that the Creator and the great Golden Retriever played and took long walks, and rested in the shade of a great tree.

Chapter 2

1. When the Creator realized the awesome duties of governing all that had been created, the Creator realized that it would not be fair to the Great Golden Retriever, so the Creator decided to create a special place called Green Valley. This was a place that some have called Eden. The Creator put two human creatures in Green Valley so they could tend and keep it. They were also responsible for taking care of the Creator's Great Golden Retriever.

2. When the Creator put the Golden Retriever in Green Valley, the Creator named him Sampson. The Creator named the humans Adam and Eve. Seeing that Eve was without a puppy, the Creator gave her a dog as well—a loving little Bulldog puppy. Thus, the family of humanity began with a Golden Retriever, a baby Bulldog, and a man and a woman.

3. Just before the Creator went on about the tasks of overseeing the cosmos, the Creator told Adam and Eve, "Go in peace.

Give love to your dogs. And, whatever you do, don't pick any apples from the tree that is in the center of the garden."

4. Time passed and the dogs and their humans were very happy in Green Valley. Then, it came to pass that Eve saw an apple had fallen from the forbidden tree. She thought to herself, " The Creator didn't say, 'Don't pick up any fallen apples.' I think the Creator only said, 'Don't *pick* from the tree any apples.'" Having created such a rationale, Eve picked up the apple and tossed it. Both the Retriever and the Bulldog scampered across the meadow in chase of the apple. The Bulldog got there first and accidentally bit into the skin of the apple as he scrambled to get it in his mouth. The apple bounced away a few feet. By then the Retriever had caught up, and quickly snatched up the apple and firmly clamped it in the corner of his mouth. Thus, juice from the apple of knowledge was immediately absorbed by both dogs. They now possessed knowledge. They both knew why the Creator did not want knowledge of this type contained in humans.

5. Instead of bringing the apple back to Eve, the dogs tried to keep it away. Both Adam and Eve began playfully chasing the dogs across the grassy fields. Soon, both the humans and the dogs were exhausted. But by now the humans were angry, not knowing why the dogs failed to release the apple.

6. Finally, Adam took a stick and began beating the two dogs. They suffered through the beating, still unwilling to give to the humans something they now knew was harmful to them. This was the first act of unconditional love.

7. At this moment the Creator appeared, and was very angry with the two humans. The Creator said: "You have inflicted harm upon a creature who only gives you love in return. You gave to them the fruit of knowledge I forbid you to ingest. Now, their great knowledge about love magnifies your ignorance. You have created a great imbalance in the Grand Scheme of Things."

8. The Creator then banished the two humans from the Green Valley. This made the Great Golden Retriever and his Bulldog companion very sad. They no longer had any humans to keep them company and to whom they could show their unconditional love.

Chapter 3

1. It came to pass that the Creator again visited the Green Valley and the two dogs told the Creator of their sadness. The Creator blessed them and said, "In the Grand Scheme of Things it will come to pass, in due time, that dogs will dwell forever with humans in a place of peace. There are things that must happen, though, before this peaceful reunion will occur."

2. The Golden Retriever asked the Creator, "But what about now? We miss our humans now. Is there not something that can be done now?"

3. The Creator spoke, "Yes. You shall go forth as a part of the Grand Scheme of Things. Your species will populate the earth and multiply and flourish. Your puppies shall be possessions of humans; some will be loved; some will be abused. The great gift of knowledge about unconditional love you acquired from the tree of knowledge will allow you to survive in the midst of hatred, evil, cruelty, and viciousness, and still feel and give love to all. Then, it will come to pass that events will unfold in the Grand Scheme of Things, so that humans finally obtain true knowledge about unconditional love. Then they will be worthy to dwell with the most loving of all creatures in a Great Green Valley forever.

Chapter 4

1. It came to pass that there was a genealogy of Sampson, the Great Golden Retriever. The first offspring was owned by Abraham, who begot Isaac, Isaac begot Jacob, and Jacob begot Judah and his brothers. The Abraham tribe favored the Sheltie and the Terrier breeds.

2. Judah begot Perez and Zerah by Tamar, Perez begot Hezron, and Hezron begot Ram. This clan tended to breed and raise Doberman dogs, and Rottweilers.

3. Ram begot Amminadaba, Amminadaba begot Nahshon, and Nahshon begot Salmon. This clan brought to prominence the Greyhound and Whippet breeds of dogs.

4. Salmon begot Boaz and Rahab, Boaz begot Obed and Ruth, Obed begot Jesse. This clan was different. They bred cats.

5. And Jesse begot David the king. David favored the collie and other herding species of dogs. David the king begot Solomon by her who had been the wife of Uriah.

6. Solomon begot Rehoboam, Rehoboam begot Abijah, and Abijah begot Asa. It was in this clan that the Great Dane species came into prominence.

7. Asa begot Jehoshaphat, Jehoshaphat begot Joram, and Joram begot Uzzian. Their dogs were the great Saint Bernard.

8. Uzziah begot Jotham, Jotham begot Ahaz, and Ahaz begot Hezehiah. And the German Shepherds were their companions.

9. Hezehiah begot Manasseh, Manasseh begot Amon, and Amon begot Josiah. The Basset Hounds were popular among this tribe.

10. Josiah begot Jeconiah and his brothers about the time they were carried away to Babylon. This clan brought forth the Yellow Retrievers.

11. And after they were brought to Babylon, Jeconiah begot Shealtiel, and Shealtiel begot Zerubbabel. After Babylon, this diverse clan gave prominence to what was called the mixed-breed mongrel dog, the most populous and loved of all dog creatures.

12. Zerubbabel begot Abiud, Abiud begot Eliakim, and Eliakim begot Azor. This clan popularized the breed of Springer Spaniels.

13. Azor begot Zadok, Zadok begot Achim, and Achim begot Eliud. This clan brought forth the breed of Pekinese.

14. Eliud begot Eleazar, Eleazar begot Matthan, and Matthan begot Jacob. This clan shared the unconditional love of the Cocker Spaniels.

15. And Jacob begot Joseph the husband of Mary, of whom was born Jesus who is called Christ. Joseph was unaware that the Golden Retriever who accompanied him and Mary on their journey to Bethlehem was a direct descendant of the Creator's first Golden, the Retriever named Sampson.

16. So all the generations from Abraham to David are fourteen generations, from David until the captivity in Babylon are fourteen generations, and from the captivity in Babylon until the

Christ are fourteen generations.

17. In each of these human generations there as a corresponding seven generations of dog. This means that 42 generations of humans produced seven times that generations of dogs. In total 294 generations of Golden Retrievers lived before the time of Jesus Christ.

Chapter 5

1. Now the birth of Jesus Christ was as follows: after His mother Mary was engaged to Joseph, before they came together, she was found with a Child of the holy spirit.

2. Then Joseph her husband, being a just man, and not wanting to make her a public example, was minded to put her away secretly. His young Golden Retriever, carrying the wisdom of Sampson in his genealogy, took long walks with Joseph as he contemplated his choices.

3. But while he was contemplating these things on his long walks, behold the spirit of the Creator spoke to him through a dream, and spoke through Joseph's trusted Golden: "Joseph, son of David, do not be afraid to take Mary as your wife, for that Puppy conceived in her womb is of the Creator's Holy Spirit."

4. "And she will bring forth a Son, and you shall call His name Jesus, for He will save His people from their sins. He will live a life which shows that humans, like the great dogs of creation, are capable of showing each other unconditional love."

5. So all this was done so that the Creator's Grand Scheme of Things might unfold and come to fruition. Dogs throughout the lands whispered into the ears of their sleeping humans that the Creator's plan was unfolding, saying:

6. "Behold, the virgin shall be with Child, and bear a Son, and they shall call his name 'Immanuel,' which is translated, 'God with us.'

Chapter 6

1. It came to pass that Jesus was born. Soon afterwards, the Retriever who lay at the edge of the manger and watched the

miracle of the childbirth, knowing that the Child was in danger, waited until Joseph was asleep. Then the Creator's voice came from the Retriever's mouth and whispered into the ear of Joseph, "Arise, take the young Child and His mother, flee to Egypt, and stay there until I bring you word; for Herod the king will seek the young Child to destroy Him."

2. The next morning the Retriever jostled Joseph awake. When he arose, he took the young Child and His mother by night and departed for Egypt.

3. When they finally arrived in Egypt, the Retriever still could smell fear in the place. Again, during a time when Joseph was sleeping, the voice of the Creator spoke though the Retriever, "Arise, take the Child and His mother to the land of Israel, for those who sought the young Child's life are dead."

Chapter 7

1. It came to pass that the young Jesus, with His companion the Golden Retriever, was walking on a journey from Galilee. The Retriever smelled the scent of the Creator and led Jesus to the banks of the river Jordan.

2. This human called John was one of the Creator's prophets. He was responsible for baptizing people and bringing them into knowledge of the Grand Scheme of Things. He baptized them by submersion in the Jordan, as they told of their evil doings and asked for forgiveness.

3. When Jesus asked to be baptized, John told Jesus: "I indeed baptize You with water unto repentance, but He who is coming after me is mightier than I, whose sandals I am not worthy to carry. He will baptize You with the Holy Spirit and fire.

4. "His winnowing fan is in his hand, and He will thoroughly clean out His threshing floor, and gather His wheat into the barn; but He will burn up the chaff with unquenchable fire."

5. John told Jesus, "I need to be baptized by You, and why are You coming to Me?"

6. Jesus answered and said to him, "Permit it to be so now, for thus it is fitting for us to fulfill all righteousness and to continue

with the Grand Scheme of Things."

Chapter 8

1. After Jesus was baptized, He was empowered with all of the knowledge necessary to fulfill His role as a human in the Grand Scheme of Things.

2. Thus it was that Sampson, the Golden Retriever, was now able to speak directly to Jesus and to converse about what was to happen in the Grand Scheme of Things. This knowledge, having dripped from the juice of the apple into the first Retriever's mouth, made the dog aware of things present and things to become.

3. "Now that your eyes are fully opened to the knowledge about the evil that humans do to dogs and other humans, what shall You do with Your life?" asked the Golden.

4. The Human called Jesus did not speak. Instead, He picked up a stick and tossed it ahead in the roadway. The Retriever instinctively scrambled to his feet and ran after the stick. He returned to Jesus and dropped it at His feet.

5. Once again the Human called Jesus tossed the stick ahead into the roadway. And once again the Retriever brought it back to Him.

6. Still not a word was spoken in response to the Retriever's question. Instead, the stick was tossed again, and again, until the Retriever was exhausted and thirsting.

7. When the Retriever could chase the stick no more, it became apparent to him that Jesus had answered his question with a very real example. That would be what Jesus would do with His life. He would give His energy in unconditional love to all, until there was nothing left to give. He would give everything for others. The Retriever learned his first lesson from his Human that day. And not a word was spoken.

Chapter 9

1. It came to pass that Jesus became a great preacher. Sampson always sat nearby in the crowds and listened to His preaching.

2. Sampson liked listening to his Human philosopher. He knew He was the most important Human ever to be born in the Grand Scheme of Things. During Sampson's Human's time, he saw his Human continually give and give, and forgive and forgive. Sampson knew he was witnessing the first Human who truly practiced unconditional love.

3. The message of Sampson's Human was simple. Love others. Give to others. Forgive others even when they hit you with a stick. Sampson's Human also performed what other humans called miracles because He made their bad bumps disappear and their broken bodies heal, and He brought humans back from the place behind the Great Gates of Heaven.

4. As Sampson watched his Human, he knew there was something that was still not right in the Grand Scheme of Things. He knew that when his Human called Jesus went to the place behind the gates, Sampson would not be able to follow.

5. One day, Sampson asked his Human, Jesus, what would have to happen so that dogs could be reunited with their humans in the place behind the Great Gates. And as was his way, the Human did not answer with words. Instead, He took Sampson into the desert and motioned for him to stay. Sampson obeyed. The hot sun began to bake down on the great dog. There was no shade nor water. But Sampson continued to obey. A few hundred yards away, Sampson saw an oasis of trees, and he could smell cooling water bubbling from the deep below the desert. But Sampson continued to sit in the sun, as directed by his Master, Jesus.

6. When night fell, there was no relief for Sampson. His stomach growled with hunger. And there was a cold night chill that pained as it whistled across his sun-scorched flesh. Yet the Golden Retriever called Sampson continued to obey his Master.

7. By the end of the third day, the once strong and vital Sampson was near death. But he remained loyal to his Master's word. He stayed in the place commanded by his Master.

8. On the morning of the fourth day, the Master returned. He looked different from how He looked before. His body was mostly

naked, and He wore a crown of thorns on His head. There were wounds on His hand and in His side.

9. "I have come for you. Sampson. My work here is done. You are the first I have returned for because you never doubted My word. Come, Sampson, I have prepared a place for you in Green Valley, the place from which all dogs originally came."

10. Sampson could barely walk, but the presence of his Master gave him renewed vitality. It was then that Sampson asked this most loving of all creations, "What must happen for dogs to be with their masters behind the Great Gates?"

11. It was then Sampson was made aware of the great truth. In the Grand Scheme of Things a descendant of the Creator's original Retriever would come to his final days and would lead a revolution in Green Valley that would compel the keeper of the gate to journey to the place behind the gates and utter the message to the Creator: "It is now. The Retriever has come. This book known as the Gospel of Sampson has been presented at the gates as proof that the prophecy is fulfilled. It will signal that the final events of the Grand Scheme of Things may commence. All good humans and all good dogs may at last be reunited in an everlasting peace. It is done."

Bo and I were incredulous as we listened to the Beagle translate the words of the missing Gospel of Sampson.

As the Beagle closed the volume, everyone in the room was silent. We had been listening so intently to each chapter and verse that none of us wanted the Beagle to stop.

"Is that all there is?" I asked. It appeared that only part of the manuscript had been read. There were still pages that the Beagle had not read.

"Oh, there's more, as you can see," responded the Beagle. "I think you've got the answers you need, though. This proves that dogs were the chosen ones and that humans were an afterthought. We have the right to be in Heaven."

"And..." he added. "You're the one who has to lead us in a revolution."

All three of them looked at me and almost in unison said, "Come on, lead us in a revolution. What exactly do you want us to do?"

"I'm not sure what I'm supposed to do. What do you think it means, 'a revolution?'"

The Beagle was exasperated at my ignorance. "It means that every dog here in Green Valley would prefer to be again with his or her human. We're relying on you. It's built into the Grand Scheme of Things that you figure out some way. We're behind you, Buster. Now tell us what to do."

"I wish I knew, guys. I wish I knew. Give me some time to think about it."

I stared at the manuscript and hoped that somehow it would make me aware of exactly what I was supposed to do. I could feel a tingling sensation around my neck and became aware that I was wearing the collar that was worn by the first Golden Retriever. It was the collar worn by the Sampson who was described in that ancient manuscript that sat before us on the floor of the Beagle's cluttered house.

It didn't make me feel like a revolutionary leader, however. But it did make me feel that I had to do whatever was necessary to make things right so I could again be with my human, Debby. If that meant I had to lead a revolution, fine!

CHAPTER 13

"That's it. We've done it. The program's ready for execution."
A group of humans huddled around Harry Hartman's computer workstation. Harry had called the meeting to demonstrate how the Revelations Program would work.

"Awesome."

"Incredible."

"I've never seen anything like it. The Creator is going to love it. It's truly a masterpiece. It's what we've been waiting for, Harry. Now you've done it."

Harry sat back in his chair and spread his arms behind his head. He knew it was a great piece of work. He basked in the praise of his associates. He never took the time to enjoy similar praise when he was working in his previous life. It was always rush, rush, onto the next project. This was different. Once it was executed, there would be no need for further work. Everything would come to a final, perfect end point. The program was quite simple. Once executed, it would enable all consciousness in the cosmos to perceive that matter was returning to its origin. Once all matter returned, there would be no perception of either time or space. The part Harry brought to the Revelations Project was the graphic perception of the Apocalypse. His graphics were more dazzling and more detailed than any of the scriptures or the prophets imagined. Ever since Harry arrived at the gates, all those involved in the project knew the end of time was near.

"This is wonderful stuff, Harry." The unfamiliar voice startled Harry from his daydreaming. It was the voice of the Creator. The Creator appeared in the form of one of the many "suits" that supervised the work of the computer room. Everyone in the room, however, knew that this was the most important "suit." The Creator had a presence that would humble the most powerful CEO. The Creator put a hand on Harry's shoulder as he looked down at the graphics displayed on the screen. He was pleased with the results.

"This is the last piece, Harry. I've been expecting it. Now I can begin the final shutdown phase of the Grand Scheme of Things."

"When will you execute the final phase command?" inquired Harry. The Creator smiled. "I already have. It's happening as we speak."

Harry got a worried look on his face. His dog, Larry, continued to send him accounts of what was going on in Green Valley. He was aware that a Golden Retriever was hot on the trail of the missing Gospel of Sampson. If it was found soon, then dogs and humans would be reunited in Heaven. If the Revelations Project was completed, then the Grand Scheme of Things would be finalized without reuniting dogs and humans.

"How long will it take?" asked Harry.

The Creator smiled. "You're worried about the dogs, aren't you? Harry, Harry. Don't you realize I am aware of everything?"

"Well, I guess you know then about my dog, Larry. He's a German Shepherd. He's in Green Valley. I miss him. I wish he was here with me." The Creator walked around the room, looking very official and very interested in all the activities that continued to happen around Harry's work area. The Creator appeared to be considering what Harry had just said.

"So, are you telling me that you are not satisfied with Heaven as it is? It's supposed to be perfect, you know."

"Well, all I meant to say was that I miss my dog. It would be a better Heaven if he were here. That's all I meant. This place is great. Don't get me wrong. I'm thankful I'm here. I just wish Larry was here with me. That's all." The Creator looked around the room and noticed that there were hundreds of workers listening to the conversation with Harry.

"How many of you had dogs in your former life?" More than eighty percent of the people raised their hands.

"How many of you miss your dogs?" All of the same hands shot into the air. The Creator smiled knowingly. "Well, well. It appears as though there is a problem here, doesn't it? Here we are on the eve of the Revelations Project, and the end of time. And here we have a vast majority of you who are not as happy as you might be."

Harry spoke up. "You're the wise Creator. Isn't it easy for You to simply change things? You can make a new rule and open the gates. Why don't You do it now before it's too late?"

The Creator sat down in a chair next to Harry and patted him gently on his leg. "Everything was created for a purpose. Everything has happened for a purpose. All of the design was perfect in the beginning. All of the design will be perfect in the ending. If you believe in the Grand Scheme of Things, you will be satisfied with the perfect harmony of the eternity that is unfolding as we speak." The Creator smiled. Harry was filled with a sense of peace and comfort. The rest of the people in the room were equally at peace. The Creator didn't change anything. But it was crystal clear that the Creator was in control of everything. Then, just as He had suddenly appeared to the Revelations Project workers, the Creator disappeared. None of the humans was worried any longer about his or her dog in the Grand Scheme of Things. But they had no idea what was going to happen.

While the workers in the Revelations Project were having their conversation with the Creator, Bo and Jose and I were still sitting on the floor in the Beagle's front room. The Beagle had reopened the manuscript and was silently reading the remainder of its contents. He was searching for additional information that we might use to help us create the revolution that was called for in the first part of the scriptures.

"What's wrong, Zack? I asked, as his expression abruptly changed. "Why are you frowning? Is there something in the manuscript that you haven't told us?" Zack didn't answer for awhile.

He grew silent and seemed to be engrossed in the strange markings on the pages of the manuscript. Then he said, "Yes. There is something I'm not sure about. It has to do with the concept of revolution."

"What do you mean?" I asked.

"Well, it says here that a Golden One will lead a revolution among the dogs of Green Valley as a sign that the final phase of the Grand Scheme of Things is coming to an end."

I still didn't have a good sense of what the Beagle was talking about. "What do you mean, 'a revolution?'" The Beagle seemed frustrated by my ignorance of history. "Goodness gracious, my good fellow. You mean to tell me you don't know about revolutions? They are the great drama of civilization. Whenever human civilization bogs down into the boring reality of dealing with difficult problems, some charismatic leader pops up and leads a revolution. It's the way humans make things change on a grand scale.

"Revolutions are the short cut alternatives to evolution. The Grand Scheme of Things was designed to follow the natural evolution of things. But that takes time. Revolutionaries are impatient. They want to make things right, and they don't want to take a lot of time doing it."

"So, what's wrong with that?" I asked. The Beagle rolled his eyes. "Revolutionaries are idealists. They aren't practical. They are willing to sacrifice everything because they think their way is better than the way things are."

"Is there anything wrong with that?"

"I suppose it depends upon what's at risk," said the Beagle.

I didn't have to think long before I realized that there was a lot at risk in my way of looking at things. Something was terribly wrong with the Grand Scheme of Things. It was difficult not to be a revolutionary Retriever if that's what had to happen to fix things. If he's caught in the right circumstances, even a mild and gentle creature can resort to revolution. I thought how curious it was in the Grand Scheme of Things that I really didn't choose to do what I now knew I had to do. I wondered if that's the way it was with the other grand revolutions. As I thought about it, revolutions seemed to be a natural cycle of evolution. But when you're caught up in the exigencies and urgencies, it seems like you're choosing and acting on the outside of things. That's the thing that continued to confound me about the Grand Scheme of Things. Every time I thought I was taking charge and being in control, I would get a glimpse of some evidence that pointed to the contrary view.

I turned to Bo and sought his counsel. "Bo, what do you think has to happen? What does all this stuff mean?"

"We've got to get a group of dogs and charge the gates," Bo said immediately. "We've got to make such a noise that it disrupts everybody and everything going on behind the gates. We've got to get the Creator to come and hear our petitions. We've got to show the Creator that we've got the lost gospel."

"How are we going to do that? What is going to make the dogs behave differently than they have up until now? What's different?"

"You're here. They know the tradition. They know a Golden is supposed to lead them so they can get an audience with the Creator. When you're ready, they'll come."

"How can you be so sure?" I asked Bo. I'd never seem him so absolutely assertive, even in our former lives.

"Think about it, Buster. Think about how much you long to see Debby and Roger. Even though there's no real measure of time here in Green Valley, we all sense the distance that is growing between where we were, and where we are now. A great number of the dogs have humans who exist behind those great and glorious gates. They long to see and feel the presence of their humans. Trust me, I know."

"You know, Bo, you're right. Imagine if we knew we'd be with our humans the moment they arrived at the gates. I know I'd be praying this very moment that circumstances would quickly bring Debby's demise. Maybe the Creator didn't want a whole bunch of dogs praying that humans would quickly die and come to the gates! That would really disrupt the Grand Scheme of

Things."

"Maybe. But I think you're giving the Creator more credit than is deserved. This is clearly one case where the Creator totally blew it! Period. And you've been chosen to bring it to the Creator's attention. That's totally awesome."

"So, let's see if we can figure out how to get all the dogs to the gate. Is there some kind of newspaper here in Green Valley? Any television? How do we communicate with everyone?"

Bo and I were so engrossed in our conversation, we almost forgot the Beagle was carefully studying and rereading the words on the manuscript.

"There is an answer to your question here in the document. It's really very easy. Listen." The Beagle began reading:

"It shall come to pass that the Golden Retriever shall position himself at the gate and wail in a tone and at a frequency that shall be so pure it shall draw to the gates all canine creatures in Green Valley who have a human dwelling apart behind the gates. These dogs shall join in the chorus, and it shall attract their humans who shall press upon the gates from inside so that the Creator shall appear, fearing that the very walls of Heaven shall tumble down. Then the Creator shall be presented with the lost gospel. Then it will be time to commence the ending of time. Then it will be time for dogs to join humans in Heaven. Thus will end for all time the structures and barriers that have separated dogs from humans in the afterlife. When this happens, there will be no stuff, no matter, present in the domain of the Creator that can be a dwelling for the evil spirit, or act as an agent of evil."

"So," Bo said, "that's why the evil one kept the manuscript hidden and protected by the Pitbull. When there is nowhere to dwell, evil will disappear into the emptiness. Evil can only exist as long as the Creator's Grand Scheme of Things is evolving into its perfect state."

"Right. And it can't be perfect, we both know," I exclaimed, "until dogs and humans can be together forever!"

"Right!" Bo repeated. "So, what are you waiting for? Let's

get to the gates. You've got some howling and wailing to do!"

As we left the Beagle's house, he shouted to us from the porch. "I'll be along as soon as I round up the rest of my crowd. I haven't had a good howling since I was a pup. I wonder if Doc will recognize my sound?"

Bo, Jose and I dashed full speed ahead toward the gates that were beginning to appear on the horizon.

When we arrived, I stood there feeling a bit sheepish. I was somewhat relieved that Saint Peter was nowhere to be found. It would have been awkward, just walking up and starting to wail.

In fact, nobody was around. Bo looked at me. "Well, go ahead. Start wailing. Make it a good one."

I cleared my throat. I was surprised at how difficult it is to make sounds just for the sake of making a sound. I didn't have anything to say. I was just supposed to howl. No, that wasn't exactly right. I was supposed to wail with feeling. I was supposed to protest.

Protest isn't about reason or logic. It's about feeling. So you don't need words. Howling like a dog is perfectly acceptable. I thought it was probably a preferable method. It's a method that human revolutionaries have only begun to understand in the course of the Grand Scheme of Things. The problem with human protests is that they confuse the need to howl with words that contain some fragments of meaning. A dog's protest is more pure and basic. It's just noise with feeling. When enough dogs start harmonizing the feeling will get more intense. When it reaches its highest point, you have a full-blown dog revolution. I don't know if anybody ever taught me this truth, but it seemed so self-evident I was sure it was true.

"Go ahead, Buster. What are you waiting for? Debby and Roger and Pam and Norm aren't getting any younger." Bo nudged me with his nose. I always hated it when he poked my ribs with his nose. It was always so wet and cold!

"Here goes nothing, Bo." I let out my best wailing howl. It was unlike anything Debby or Roger had ever heard, I was sure of that. I wasn't used to howling. I'm a barker. I'm crisp, determined, and sometimes ferocious sounding, especially when the mail is delivered by the red, white and blue truck.

At first my wail sounded a bit empty and hollow. Bo soon joined in and we became a duet. Then other dogs started appearing, in twos and threes. Soon there were groups and bunches. I continued the one wailing note that seemed to be the pitch pipe for the growing chorus of wailing. Then, almost as though it was magic, we were aware that all the creatures living in Green Valley were united in a chorus of howling. It was awesome. Bo looked over at me and smiled, without even breaking his sound. It was a magnificent moment, a sense of oneness among all of the dogs that had been separated from their humans in the afterlife since the beginning of time. It was the moment they had waited for.

Nobody was sure, though, that the howling would achieve the effect we wanted. There was no sign of Saint Peter. There was no chorus of angels. There were no signs of anything.

Bo nudged me. He stopped howling long enough to say. "Look Buster. Look at the gates and the walls. There's something happening behind them. There is an energy field that is pushing on the walls. I'll bet it's the humans. We're reminding them of something from the past that is missing in their ideal afterlife. We're awakening the humans. It's their collective spirit."

Bo was so excited. I had no idea what he was babbling about because the sound of the howling was deafening. But I could see that something was causing the gates and the wall to shake. I was fearful that the sound was so powerful it would knock down the gates, and we'd make the Creator really mad. But it was too late to stop things now. I just kept howling, looking for some sign that we were producing results. I thought about how other revolutionaries and protesters probably get so caught up in their own actions that they get fearful and worried about whether they're going to produce anything but disaster and chaos. Then, when it seemed like we'd been howling forever, a loud voice rose above the noise of the dogs. "Hush. Hush," it said. Almost instantly, all of the dogs seemed to disappear into nowhere. The only remaining sound was the booming wailing of Jose. I was startled when I realized that his voice was almost as powerful as the Creator's. I glared at Jose as he remained defiant in his protest. Once again the little creature showed his tremendous courage. I caught his eye and motioned for him to stop. Then it was perfectly silent. It was just Bo, Jose and me, alone at the gates. I was frightened and whispered to the two of them.

"Who was that? Where did everybody go?"

Bo was shaking, "That voice was the Creator. I think we got the Creator's attention, Buster. You did it. He heard."

"But what am I supposed to do now, you guys?" I responded.

"Beats me, Buster. I thought you knew."

Jose stood in front of us, trying to show us that he wasn't even afraid of the Creator.

CHAPTER 14

Bo and I were awestruck by what appeared in the sky above the gates blocking the entry to Heaven. There was a cobalt blue swirl of stuff that looked like huge ocean waves rolling endlessly over and over themselves. It grew and shrunk in size. I felt like we were looking at the sun through a lens that screened out the brilliance of what would otherwise be pure light. It was a cloud of shapeless blue energy, and it must be intelligent if it spoke the words a moment ago. Both Bo and I trembled with fear. Jose stood his ground and let out a low rumbling growl.

"Creator, Sir…" I hesitated for a moment, thinking how stupid it seemed to be, talking to a cloud. But there was something about the cloud that made me feel it was O.K. I had no doubt it was the Creator. I just wasn't sure how to address Him.

"Sir, we've done what the missing book said we were supposed to do if we wanted to make things right in the Grand Scheme of Things. We rallied at the gates and created a protest that would bring your presence to us. I'm sorry we made such a disturbance. This is my first revolution, and frankly I'm certain there must be a better way to get someone's attention than staging a revolution. Although, with all due respect, it did seem to work, didn't it?" I caught myself thinking that I was beginning to sound like a braggart. The cloud changed from blue to yellow to white light so brilliant it almost blinded us. Then it grew intensely blue again, like the ocean on a clear, sunny summer afternoon.

We heard a firm calming voice, as though it were coming from a human standing right in front of us. "Good, dog. Good Buster. Good dog, Good Bo."

I looked at Bo. He was as startled as I was to hear the Creator speaking in such familiar and gentle tones. I didn't want to tell Bo, but if anybody had asked me, I'd say the Creator's voice sounded exactly like Debby's. But I was sure it was just my imagination.

"You've done your jobs," the voice went on. " You've found the lost words, and you fulfilled what was written. The events that were planned in the Grand Scheme of Things continue to come to pass. It is now time to bring all good things back to perfection, as they were in the beginning."

"Does that mean that when Debby comes to the gates I can be with her in Heaven?" I asked respectfully.

"It means that and much more, Buster. It means that the remaining emptiness of evil will be driven from the Grand Scheme of Things."

"I'm not sure what You mean, Sir. Why are You driving out *emptiness*? Why is it evil?" The voice was soothing as it took what seemed like great care to explain complex things so they could be understood by intelligent dogs.

"Before the beginning of time, everything was perfect and whole. There was no space. And because there was no space, there was no stuff. I alone was aware of the wonderful stuffness of beingness in all of its wholeness."

"So why did you create emptiness?" I asked, hoping it wasn't as dumb a question to ask the Creator as it sounded. The cloud seemed to vibrate, as though responding physically to my comment. I sensed it might have thought it a funny question to come from a dog.

"Ah, Buster. Your time with Roger made you perceptive. You ask the right questions. Emptiness is the essential ingredient of the Grand Scheme of Things. When stuff is set apart from stuff with emptiness, then it creates the possibility that things can be seen as separate and distinct from the whole. It is emptiness that makes stuff possible. It is the emptiness of the clay pot that makes it a useful container of stuff."

I didn't want to tell the Creator that I was already in over my head with this conversation, but I figured it couldn't hurt my chances of soon being reunited with Debby if I just listened politely, smiled, and nodded like I understood. I nudged Bo to do the same thing. His head immediately began bobbing up and down in agreement.

"Well," said the Creator's voice, "creating emptiness enabled awareness of stuff. And when this happened in the Grand Scheme of Things, the sense of evil was born and the great struggle between Good and Evil could take place."

I shook my head. I didn't understand, and I knew it was important to at least have a general sense of what the Creator was saying. Then I'd be able to talk intelligently with Roger when we visited one of the philosopher walls that surely existed behind the gates.

"I can tell you're having difficulty," the Creator said, reading our minds. "I've jumped too far ahead in My story. Let Me backtrack. Once things could be separated, it was wonderful to imagine and create all sorts of stuff, like the heavens, the earth, the oceans, and the trees. All of this stuff was possible because I could mix it with emptiness—meaning I could set it apart from other things by adding what you call space, and I call emptiness."

He paused, as if to give us a bit of time to think about how things were separated by space. That wasn't the hard part. What was hard to imagine was when there was no space between anything, and everything was crowded into one point.

"When I finally created humans so they could be enjoyed by dogs, and other creatures, I knew that it would come to pass that evil would come into conflict with the essential goodness of things that existed in the Grand Scheme of Things."

"Why?" I asked curiously.

"Because when I created humans, I wanted them to come as close as possible to knowing and feeling the wholeness of the stuffness of beingness as I, the Creator, did. But I didn't want them to start becoming aware of this potential power, so I withheld knowledge of this awareness. But, I also had to create the opportunity for knowing, because it was essential to the Grand Scheme of Things."

"Why?"

"Because there had to be the opportunity to do wrong, or there would be no way of knowing that everything was innocent and right."

"So, what does the story of the apple and the beating of the dogs have to do with emptiness and evil?"

"When I banished the humans from Green Valley for beating the dogs, it also created their awareness of the pureness of unconditional love. I put distance, meaning emptiness, between the humans and their dogs."

"So, how did this cause evil to grow and expand in the Grand Scheme of Things?"

"Good question, Buster. Good question. A basic law of existence was created. It goes something like this. When a human feels a sense of emptiness, the human will do everything possible to fill the emptiness."

"Is that so bad?" I asked, thinking that it sounded like the right way to approach things.

"The problem, Buster, is that once the emptiness is created, once the separateness is created in the events of the Grand Scheme of Things, the best thing humans can do is to accept the small separateness, and emptiness. And to have faith that something other than their personal efforts will eventually fill the emptiness. But that's not what they do."

"Why not?" I asked.

"Emptiness takes on a life of its own. That's what I have instructed humans to call evil."

"Evil is the disease of emptiness in the human spirit. It's what put space and distance between the original wholeness of the non-self, and the self that becomes focused on itself as stuff."

It was almost as though the Creator realized he'd totally overloaded us with knowledge about all this stuffness of beingness. He ended the conversation, almost abruptly, with some final words:

"The stuffness of beingness is oneness. Evil is the distance between, and the boundaries around, the stuff we have separated from the original wholeness. Human pain and suffering come from trying to fill the original emptiness with more emptiness. The more humans have done this, the more evil has expanded in the Grand Scheme of Things. Now it is time to collapse the space and distance of stuff back into the original wholeness."

We could tell that the Creator was withdrawing from our awareness, because the rolling blue waves of light began to fade.

"Wait, sir. Just one more question. Is there anything else I'm supposed to do to complete my part of this Grand Scheme of Things?"

"Yes," said the voice, now very faint, "You will soon know. Listen to your own being. It will make you aware, as it always has, ever since dogs first ate of the fruit of knowledge."

"And, please, would you stop addressing Me as Sir?"

I looked at Bo and Jose. They both shrugged.

"Certainly we will, Creator, but why?" The cloud, that moments ago had nearly faded away, formed into a human image for a split second, then disappeared. I couldn't believe what I saw. I wasn't sure whether Bo or Jose saw it either.

Now there was a strange hush surrounding the gates, which Bo and Jose and I were amazed to find had opened wide. We were free to enter. There was no sign of Saint Peter, so we cautiously made our way through into Heaven. At last.

I was still puzzled by what I'd seen when the cloud seemed to take human form. I look at Bo and Jose, half embarrassed to tell them, but I couldn't keep it to myself. "Do you know what? I think I saw the image of God."

Bo responded. "Me too, Buster, it was awesome."

"What did you see? I didn't see anything," asked Jose.

"Who do you think the Creator looks like?" I asked Bo.

We answered in unison.

Bo said, "Pam!"

I said, "Debby!"

CHAPTER 15

Roger was running around the Soquel High School track when my awareness struck him. He stopped almost in full stride, as my message began to be absorbed by his consciousness. I could tell he was surprised to be so clearly aware of me during the midday. Ordinarily, it was easier to make contact with him when he slept. For some reason, humans are more receptive to things when they sleep. That's too bad, when you think about it. So much of what is going on around humans is struggling to enter their awareness, but humans get so preoccupied with stuff they block out a lot of the important messages. They especially block those messages that don't come in the form of television, radio, newspapers, phone calls, meetings, memos, and face-to-face conversation.

I was glad that Roger and I agreed before I jumped into the tunnel of light that he'd keep an open mind and consciousness so that we'd have some special channel to use. I was finding out from talking with other dogs that it really isn't easy to communicate with humans across the barrier of time.

I really had a scoop for Roger this time. I was certain he was going to be excited to know that I was fixing the Grand Scheme of Things. It wasn't yet quite right, from my perspective, but I was getting there. Roger would be especially pleased to know that I'd had a conversation with the Creator. I decided not to tell him, though, that the Creator looked remarkably like Debby!

When I was sure Roger was conscious of me, I began jabbering about all that had happened since our last visit. I couldn't remember what I'd told him, but I was sure he hadn't been aware of the missing gospel or the revolution I'd created at the gates. I quickly updated him, then got to the heart of what I wanted to tell him about the Creator. I knew it would give him a lot to think about as he took his runs and his lonely walks without me.

"The Creator even used the terms you used, Roger. She said 'the wonderful stuffness of beingness.' So you're on the right track, Roger."

"What do you mean, 'She?'"

"Oh, yeah, that's really interesting. The Creator's a She, not a Him. I saw Her. I'm positive."

"Well, what did She look like, Buster?"

I didn't want to tell Roger that She looked exactly like Debby! That might have spooked him. Not that he would have treated Debby any differently, but it might have made things a bit awkward. I imagine it would be difficult for any human, Roger included, to live with somebody they thought looked like God the Creator."

"Oh, you know, just a nice woman. Probably like Debby's mom!"

I could almost hear Roger chuckle as he tried to envision Verla as the Creator. He knew she was a conservative Christian. He probably wondered how she might react to the thought of God being a She, especially a She that looked like her. It would probably mortify her!

"What do you think about the notion that evil is a result of humans being aware of the space and distance between things? She said evil is the product of emptiness."

"Sounds kind of strange and far-fetched to me, Buster. Are you sure that's what the Creator meant? Maybe She was simply speaking metaphorically?"

"I don't think so. She said that when She created stuff She mixed pure oneness with emptiness. What do you make of that?" I asked Roger.

I could tell he was thinking about the question, because I sensed he'd again started slowly jogging around the outside lane of the track.

"You know, Buster, that's an interesting concept. When humans build stuff like houses, and office buildings, and cars, and televisions, we use space to separate the parts. And when the whole thing is assembled, it contains space and emptiness. So in that sense, emptiness is essential to the separateness of stuff. Not a bad concept. I'll have to think about it more. So what else did the Creator tell you about the Grand Scheme of Things?"

"She told me a lot about how now that the prophecy of the Retriever has been fulfilled, it was time to get rid of all the emptiness in the wholeness of beingness. What do you think She meant by that? She said that people become evil, and that evil grows, to the degree that the beingness of humans is filled with emptiness."

Roger thought about that concept for a long time. It seemed to mean more to him than it initially meant to me. Then I sensed how it was understood by him.

"Buster, that's really a curious notion. I think it's some kind of metaphor for talking about human feelings and using the same language as the physical universe."

"What do you mean?"

"Well, it's like this Buster. A lot of the humans who are studying the physics of the universe are saying that the whole universe is expanding. But they also predict it is someday going to collapse back onto itself and shrink back to its original starting point. Now the universe is so vast, it's impossible for anybody to really comprehend the magnitude of how this is going to happen and what will exist, or cease to exist, once it is accomplished. But it does seem so consistent with what the Creator told you about the Grand Scheme of Things. I can imagine that when everything collapses back onto itself, a lot of space will be eliminated. There won't be much room for emptiness when the whole scheme is concluded."

"So, what does that have to do with human feelings and evil?" I asked.

"Well, I got a bit sidetracked with my explanation. What I started to say was that when the Creator fashioned the existence

of humans from the pure oneness of beingness, there was a necessary separation from the pure oneness. When humans became
aware of the separateness, they did what was necessary to fix the
feeling of being separate. But in so doing, they also added more
emptiness."

"What happens when humans add more emptiness? How do
they add emptiness?"

"It's often a vicious cycle. They start feeling the pain of being less than whole. So they try to acquire something or achieve
something that they think will make the pain go away. Sometimes they even start thinking it is their responsibility to do things
to make their lives meaningful."

"Then what happens?"

"It depends. Some humans listen carefully to the voice from
within that continually keeps them connected with the wholeness and oneness of beingness. Some humans call this connection prayer, meditation, centeredness, or spirituality."

"What do others do who can't hear the voice from within?"

"They often do many strange things to avoid feeling the pain
of emptiness. They pretend that if they get enough money the
pain of emptiness will go away."

"What's wrong with that?"

"Well, there are certain things that naturally follow. Some
people get so obsessed with trying to use some other stuff to fix
the pain that they do things that hurt other people. When they
hurt other people, or they hurt themselves, they usually end up
doing things that many religions and philosophers call evil."

"You mean that the purpose of evil is to help people fix the
pain caused by the sense of emptiness they feel?"

"Yes, I think that's why the Creator told you that evil grows
stronger as humans become more distant from the original oneness of being. That's why stuff is stuff. It's separated from other
stuff, and it's separate from oneness."

It was beginning to make sense, this prophecy that I was a
part of fulfilling. I was curious what Roger would make out of the

Creator's description of what was about to happen.

"What do you think about the Creator bringing all of this stuffness to an end? Have you ever given much thought to that?" I asked Roger.

"Sure. You remember that time at the wall when we talked about that beingness?"

"Yes."

"I said that all good things had to come to an end. What I meant was that even in the Grand Scheme of Things, it was going to end. But what I have yet to understand is, why? Now what you are telling me makes some sense. The Creator's scheme is perfect. Once everything has been fully created and expanded to its fullness, then the wholeness is perfectly aware of its wholeness. Once that has been accomplished, it can end."

"But what is an ending?"

"I think it's the complete awareness of beingness."

"Oh," I thought to myself.

I turned again to the question of evil and asked Roger, "what does the Creator mean that there will be a final elimination of evil. Is evil a force, like the Creator?"

"I don't think so, not the way you say the Creator described evil. I think She told you something I've never thought about until now. Evil is the natural product of creating emptiness and space in the universe and in the personality of each individual human. The human awareness of the emptiness is what creates the potential for evil. When the Creator eliminates space and separateness of beingness, evil is naturally squeezed out of the Grand Scheme of Things."

"So, what about all the human theologies you talked about with me at the wall, when we talked about evil people going to some place called Hell. What do you think that's all about, especially in light of what I just learned from the Creator?"

"I don't know, Buster. I'll give it some more thought. But, off the top of my head, I say that it is surely possible that some people become so empty, so filled with fixes for the pain of separation from wholeness with beingness, that they virtually expand into nothingness. Maybe that's what this theological concept of Hell is all about."

"Is it a real place? Is there a real Evil One who tortures people for eternity? Is it the place where Bo says all the cats have to go?"

Roger laughed. I could tell he missed taking his walks to the wall with me. He could see that I'd gotten a little sloppy with my thinking. Bo was a great companion, and we had great talks, but he was no substitute for Roger.

"I think that there doesn't have to be an Evil One for people to be tortured. Emptiness is a torture that can be independent of any being. But if some people think there is an Evil One, then for them it is a real thing."

"What do you think, Roger? Is there an Evil One?"

"Hey, Buster, you're the guy on the other side. Why don't you do some sniffing around and see if you can't find out about such things? After all, you've got nothing but time for such adventures. I've got to get my stuff organized here while I still can. Then I can join you at the gates."

Before I fully retreated from Roger's consciousness and left him to the solitude of his afternoon run, I assured him I was going to do exactly as he suggested.

"Take care, Roger. I'm going to take you up on your suggestion. Bo and I will sniff around a bit and see what we can find out. I'll keep in touch."

I smiled as I again became aware of my own surroundings. Here I was, roaming freely around in the area behind the once forbidden gates of Heaven. There was time for Bo and me to kill before Roger and Debby and Pam and Norm joined us here. We might as well look around and see if we could find the Evil One and his place called Hell. It was then that I realized that I'd just gotten the answer to the question I asked the Creator. It was clear that such a search was also a part of the prophecy I was destined to fulfill.

CHAPTER 16

B o and I felt really wonderful, wandering through the streets and back alleys of the magnificent place called Heaven. It was great to see that all the dogs that lived separately in Green Valley were now with their humans in Heaven. But many still lived in Green Valley, primarily because their humans hadn't yet come to Heaven. Sadly, some dogs discovered that their former humans had become so empty that they didn't make the journey to the gates.

Fortunately, as the Grand Scheme of Things drew to a conclusion, many of the dogs who were without humans were able to wander into Heaven and find a human who matched their unique personalities. Now Heaven was truly Heaven!

And what about the Pitbull? An incredible thing happened shortly after dogs were able to enter Heaven. It came to pass that the Pit finally wandered past the gates, curious about why so many dogs wanted to be with humans. He also was tracking the scent of Jose, a smell he would not ever forget. It led him to the house of Jose and his priest human. At first all the Pit could think about was exacting his revenge on the tenacious little warrior. From his hiding place outside Jose's home, the Pit observed the loving relationship between Jose and his human. As he watched, Freddie began to realize what he had missed. He lay silent in the shrubs and began sobbing. The priest heard the awful wailing and began to search for the source of such a discordant sound in this blissful place. He pushed back the bushes and saw the Pit, sad and vulnerable. Compassionately, he reached down and picked up the Pit. Reflexively, Freddie bristled, ready to fight. Then he just relaxed in the embrace of this loving human. The priest carried the Pit into the house. Jose jumped to his feet in disbelief as he saw his old enemy.

Jose could tell that his priest human had extendeded his love to the Pit. Jose reluctantly swaggered across the floor and approached Freddie. This time, though, Jose licked him right across his face! And, guess what? The Pit did the same thing! Now the three of them will live together forever! Is there any doubt that there really is a Grand Scheme of Things?

Bo and I lay peacefully beneath a beautiful spreading shade tree in what had to be the central area of Heaven, I looked over at him and smiled. He no longer doubted the Grand Scheme of Things was perfect. He was the one who had told me the story about Jose and the Pit becoming family.

"I've been thinking, Bo. We've both got some time on our hands until our humans arrive, how about going on a little adventure?"

Bo opened his eyes just wide enough to get a look at my face to see if I was really serious or just passing the time.

"Like what kind of adventure?" he muttered, again closing his eyes. He obviously wasn't too thrilled with the idea. The quest for the manuscript had been exciting enough for him.

I persisted. "Come on, Bo. Don't be so lazy. What about trying to find out about the place we heard the other dogs in Green Valley call the Afterlife of Cats?"

Bo's eyes opened wide, and he sat up quickly. "Are you crazy? Why would you want to do that? Why would any dog in his right mind wonder about the cat afterlife?"

"Well, Bo. I've been thinking. It doesn't seem fair that while dogs can get into Heaven, I have yet to see any cats. Doesn't it seem strange that as the Grand Scheme of Things evolves, it doesn't include cats? I mean, Debby might be sad if she got here and there's no opportunity to be with Bosley. He's pretty much a part of her life, too!"

Bo sneezed. It was as if he was allergic to even the thought of being around cats. I continued to press the idea of the adventure, but Bo still resisted. Finally, I stood up and headed down the roadway toward the front gates. I knew once Bo saw I was determined, he'd join me, and I was right. He stood up, stretched, then shook himself all over to get the kinks out. Even though we both knew we were simply images of our former bodies, the rituals were still very much a part of how we imagined ourselves. I smiled as Bo joined me at my side.

"I don't know why I let you talk me into these things," he scoffed.

"I do, Bo. Do I have to constantly remind you that you were assigned to be my guardian angel?'

"It's more like I'm your watch dog, Buster." Then, from out of nowhere, we heard a familiar booming voice.

"Hey, Mr. Golden. Where are you going? Wait for me."

We both stopped and turned around. I heard Bo growl, "Oh no, it's the mouse dog with the lion's voice." Sure enough, there was Jose.

I didn't tell Bo that I was glad to see Jose again. We'd been through so much together, I really had grown fond of the little fellow. But I wasn't sure if it was a good idea for him to accompany us on this adventure.

"Hey, Jose. I heard about you and the Pit becoming friends. Is that true?"

"Sí, Señor Buster. I couldn't believe it when it happened. Freddie's really a pretty good hombre. I've grown to love him. I don't even mind sharing my human with him. Do you know what he told me, Señor Buster?"

"No. What?"

"He said I was the toughest dog he'd ever fought with in his entire life."

"Is that right?" I responded. I was kind of hoping that Jose would say that the Pit thought I was a great fighter. But I knew that wasn't true. I was a lover, not a fighter. If it hadn't been for Jose's courage, the Pit would have prevailed, and none of us, including the Pit, would have been able to enjoy Heaven.

"Where you going?" Jose asked as he realized we were headed off on a mission.

Bo responded curtly, with an ominous tone he felt would discourage Jose from pressing to join us. "We're going to explore Cat Hell. It's no place for you. They'd think you're a nice mouse morsel."

Bo didn't realize Jose considered those words a challenge to his machismo. "Señor Bo. I am not afraid of any cat, even a big lion cat. You have forgotten so soon who was afraid of the Pit. It was not this hombre, señor. Remember that!" Jose stood tall as he boomed back his response.

"I am ready to accompany you, Señor Buster. What are we waiting for?"

"O.K., little fella. You made your point. Let's not make it a big deal. You can come. Right, Bo?"

I glared at Bo, to reinforce Jose's point. There was no courage lacking in Jose. He'd be a match for any hostile cat, I was sure of that.

Bo grumbled. "O.K. If you say so."

So we again headed toward the gates. I was hoping that Saint Peter could give us some help with directions.

Peter was sitting at his desk outside the gates. He looked up as the three of us came through the dog door that appeared in the gates shortly after the changes occurred in the Grand Scheme of Things. It was the first time I'd seen Peter since the protest, and I sensed he was still having a hard time accepting the new order.

"Hey, Peter," I called to him. "How are things going? We were wondering if you could help us with some directions."

Peter looked up from his computer screen and scoffed. "Where might I direct you? God forbid that I say where I'd like to direct you!"

"Tsk, tsk, Peter. Things change. Even in the grand scheme. Remember, until the end all things are in a state of evolution. That's what the Creator Herself told me."

"What do you mean, 'Herself?' Are you being disrespectful?"

I could tell Peter had never gotten a close look at the Creator, so I didn't want to disrupt his view of things. It never occurred to me that the Creator always takes the shape and form that represent the most loving relationship known to the perceiver.

"Sorry. A slip of the tongue. I meant the Creator Himself. Seriously, Peter, can you give us some sense of where we might look if we wanted to explore where cats go in the afterlife?"

Bo cynically added, "Yeah, Peter. You know, Cat Hell!"

Peter tipped back his chair and put his arms behind his head. He smiled knowingly. "There's no special place for them. Cats go anywhere they want to go in the afterlife. They just find somewhere other than Heaven or Green Valley. I'm afraid I can't tell you any special place to look."

"Suppose my friend Bosley died since I left him in the former life. Where would I find him?" I asked. I thought that it was possible Bosley was dead, especially since I had no idea of how much cat time had lapsed since my journey through the Door of Light. And especially since I was no longer there to protect him from the black cat down the street!

"Beats me. He's probably somewhere in the Great Emptiness."

I raised my eyebrows as I repeated Peter's words, "The Great Emptiness?" Based upon all I had learned about evil and emptiness and the ending of space, I began to reconsider whether I wanted to undertake such an adventure. But then, if Bosley was going to get caught up in the Great Emptiness when the end came, I could imagine that he would be squeezed into nothingness, and that didn't sound fair, in the Grand Scheme of Things.

"Where does one find this Great Emptiness?" I inquired, half hoping Peter would tell us that it was impossible, so we could call off our journey. But in the back of my mind I also realized that for some strange reason known only to the Creator, I was destined to make this trip as a part of the prophecy.

"How did you find these gates?" responded Peter.

"Well, we just started thinking that's where we want to be and they appeared."

"It looks like you've just answered your own question, Mr. Buster. Start thinking about it and you'll find yourself there. God only knows why you'd think such thoughts. Good day."

Bo and Jose and I looked around and Peter and the gates were gone. Now that we were determined to find the Great Emptiness, it seemed quite capable of finding us!

As we walked along, darkness gathered around us. It wasn't the ordinary gray darkness that was part of the natural cycles of Green Valley and Heaven. It was dark, dark, darkness. Darker than we'd ever seen before. All we could see of each other were our glowing eyes. It was really spooky.

Bo came to a stop. So did Jose. Jose began his low growling.

"I don't know how we got here, but I know we're here," said Bo. "If this isn't the Great Emptiness, then nothing is. And I've got that itching sensation in my nose. There are cats around here. That's for sure."

Maybe Bo was right, but I couldn't see them. Suddenly little dots of light appeared everywhere, as far as I could see. It was as though I was lying on the deck of our Wixson Street house, looking up at the sky filled with twinkling stars. But it was different, because there were pairs of little stars. As I looked more carefully, I saw they were actually little pairs of eyes. Cat eyes. The cats were literally swarming in this Great Emptiness like a great buzzing of bees.

Jose's deep voice was trembling as he watched the eyes swirling everywhere. "Señor Buster, this is really spooky. So many cats. But they have nowhere to go and they only have their eyes. What do you think they do?"

Just as Jose spoke, a large swirl of eyes darted in his direction, as though they sensed he was a dog and an unwelcome visitor to this Great Emptiness. As if to signal that they were about to attack, the emptiness was filled with the sounds of angry, dog hating screeches and shrieks. Both Bo and I thought we were about to see the end of Jose, and perhaps us as well. We closed ranks on either side of Jose and prepared to defend ourselves. Then, without any warning, an eerie voice from nowhere said "Hush, hush," and the pairs of eyes disappeared instantly. We suddenly sensed the fullness of this place that Peter called the Great Emptiness.

"What was that?" exclaimed Bo. We were sure it wasn't the same voice that had quieted the dogs who had been protesting outside the Gates of Heaven.

"Who are you?" I barked into the darkness.

"Don't worry. You have nothing to fear. There's too much of you left. You're safe. There's not much space to invade in any of you dogs."

"Who are you?" I asked again, more loudly, to try and intimidate something that I couldn't see, but could feel as much as any human I'd ever scented in my former life. I could smell an evil that I'd never smelled before. It was nauseating. Had I been contained in my former body, I would have lost the contents of my stomach. But it was bad enough just experiencing the sensation, even without my former body.

"Some humans see me as the Evil One. My associates call me Ace. My enemies have a whole bunch of names for me. Some names even embarrass me to say. You can just call me Ace."

Then out of the darkness there appeared the image of the blackest, most evil-looking cat I'd ever seen. Only it wasn't the size of a cat: it was twice the size of Bo and Me. Jose's mouth fell wide open as he looked up at the awesome black cat who preferred to be called Ace!

Bo whispered to me under his breath, "This is really great, Buster. Why couldn't you have been content to just rest up and get ready for Debby's arrival at the gates? Now what are we going to do?"

CHAPTER 17

The more we gazed at the enormous black cat called Ace the lighter everything became around us, as though we were being so absorbed in the darkness that we were able to see things more clearly. I thought that maybe we were developing those cats' eyes, that can see so clearly in the dark. I glanced over at Bo and Jose just to make sure that wasn't the case. And it wasn't. They still had dog eyes. It was an illusion, I thought to myself. Everything was still pitch-black. We were just getting more accustomed to the lack of light.

Ace started circling us, like we were his long awaited prey. He began to speak in a soft purr that was at once both annoying and frightening:

"Well, well. The Great Golden Retriever has finally arrived. It certainly took you long enough to get here. I guess that means, though, that the Creator's plan for bringing the Grand Scheme of Things to its ending is about to commence. Unless, of course, I have my way with this beautiful Golden Retriever."

Ace continued to circle the three of us, purring and letting his red eyes flash, like flames flickering in a cavern of molten stone.

"Careful," cautioned Bo. "Obviously he's been expecting us, Buster. He seems to know all about you. Do you have any idea what he's talking about?"

I shook my head as I whispered to Bo and Jose, "I don't have the slightest idea—it sounds like Ace knows something about the prophecy that the Beagle forgot to translate for us."

"Oh, great. That's just great! Wait until I see the Beagle next time."

Jose interjected. "If, you ever see him again, Señor Bo."

Ace let out a great screech that must have echoed to the farthest reaches of the Great Emptiness. "You mean you don't know why you're here, Buster? You've got to be kidding! Even Goldens aren't that stupid."

Ace seemed to relish the feline myth of intellectual superiority over dogs. I was glad Bosley wasn't that way. I felt sad that unless we did something with this Ace fellow, not only was Bosley doomed to a fate separate from Debby in Heaven, but he was going to go down the cosmic tubes with this evil thing as well. I started growling and showing my teeth. Bo and Jose did the same. If the cat wanted a fight, he was going to get the best we had to offer.

But as it turned out, Ace wasn't looking for a fight. What he wanted was to make a deal. And what a deal it was.

"Relax, you stupid creatures. I'm not going to attack you. If I wanted to, I'd consume all the emptiness you've got. But that wouldn't do me much good, and it certainly wouldn't make any of you feel much better. None of us would win in that fight. No, I've got a better idea. Why don't you let me show you a much better alternative?"

"Like what?" I asked cautiously, as I relaxed from my fighting posture.

"Come over here, Buster. You too, Bo and Jose. Take a look into these doorways. What do you see?" The three of us obediently did as the cat instructed. When I looked, I could see Debby and Roger and Bosley sitting before the fireplace, just finishing dinner and enjoying the warmth of the evening fire. I felt a lump in my throat and a strong impulse to jump immediately through the door. I watched Bo and Jose and could tell they saw familiar scenes from the former lives as well. Jose didn't seem as impressed, probably because his human was already in Heaven.

"Hey, don't be afraid to show your feelings. That's what this is all about. There is only one thing that separates you from those familiar scenes. Do you know what it is?"

"No. What?" I asked defensively.

"Distance. Distance is simply space. That's the stuff of the past. I'm here to tell you that you don't have to leave it if you don't want to."

"What do you mean? We know we can't go back. They'll be here soon enough. That's what Heaven is all about."

"Oh, sure. That's what the Creator told you, isn't it? She didn't tell you that Heaven is going to change when all of the stuffness of beingness returns to oneness. Then there will be no need for Heaven. Don't you see? Heaven is just a continuation of the illusion of stuffness. That's why you want it to last forever. I don't blame you. So do I. But when the Creator eliminates all the separateness, and eliminates all space that separates stuff, it's going to be good-bye selfness and good-bye stuffness. You're just going to be a part of the Creator's little black blob."

"So, what are you telling us? If we go back through these doors we'll be with our humans forever?"

Ace smiled in a sinister way. "Precisely."

"What's in it for you, Ace?" I asked. "I can see you aren't doing this out of the kindness of your heart, or out of your love for dogs."

"Oh, you're absolutely right on that count, Golden Boy. I want you to go through that door because if you do, it will be immediately known to all of the dogs in Green Valley and all who are about to arrive in the future. Instead of lingering, waiting for humans to get to the gates, they'll all learn that they can run headlong over here and through my doorways back into the past. There are still enough opportunities to keep a sufficient volume of stuffness back in the past. The more stuff that returns to the past, the more difficult it will be to end the Grand Scheme of Things."

Ace was impassioned with rage as he continued his explanation. "You see, canine beasts, I exist only to the degree that space and distance are created between the Creator's beginning and the boundaries of all the stuff that has been created. If enough stuff is created, then it will finally snap the connection with the primal bond of wholeness and oneness that once existed. Then, if you will pardon the use of a cliché human expression, I will have successfully divided and conquered."

As I continued to listen to the diabolical nonsense that the cat was jabbering, I found that it seemed not to matter in the least. All I could focus on was the wonderful sense of connection I felt with the scene I viewed through the door. It was almost more tempting than I could resist. I didn't care how I got rejoined with Debby. I was ready. But something inside held me back.

Ace edged ever closer to me as I watched and longed to return to the scene below. He continued to whisper in my ear, "Go ahead. You can have it if you want. I guarantee you'll love it." Then I felt a push against my side, as if Ace was trying to shove me off into an abyss. I stiffened my legs. He bumped against me, and quickly backed a few steps away, almost embarrassed at my discovering his not so gentle urging. Then it occurred to me. What would happen if I could push Ace through the same doorway?

"Ace, look. It's starting to happen. All of the stuff is starting to come together. It's too late. The ending is already well under way. Look."

A startled look washed across the cat's face. He rushed to the doorway, not thinking that I was planning any trick. The moment he looked into the doorway, I made a run at his huge black rump and pushed it as hard as I could. At that precise moment, everything changed. A horrible screech filled the Great Emptiness. The cat called Ace plunged downward into the scene I'd been viewing below.

Instantly all of the darkness disappeared and the Great Emptiness was filled with millions of cats, of all kinds, as far as the eye could see. Instead of swimming in a great void, they were now aware that there were places to go in the afterlife. They headed for Green Valley and the places beyond the Gates of Heaven. I could hear cries of delight as humans reunited with their cats.

Bo and Jose were stunned. Bo started sneezing. "I guess I better get used to it. It looks like this evolving Grand Scheme of Things also includes cats. What next, Jose? What next?"

Jose swirled around and pretended to be fighting a great bull in an imaginary bull ring in Mexico. "I don't know, señor. Hey,

Señor Buster, where do bulls go in the afterlife?" The three of us started laughing. That was one question I wasn't going to ask, at least not yet. It occurred to me that once again I did my part in completing the final events in this Grand Scheme of Things. I was aware, too, of what was happening with Roger and Debby and Bosley at that precise moment.

"Screeeeech...screech. Meooooooow." Roger and Debby sat up in bed almost simultaneously. They looked at each other. "What was that?" Debby asked.

Roger muttered as he put his head back down on the pillow. "It's midnight. I think that terrible black cat just met his Maker, or maybe I'm just doing some wishful thinking."

"Good night, Roger. See you in the morning. I miss Buster. He'd be out on the balcony barking by now, wouldn't he?"

In the moment between Debby's question and Roger's response, I transmitted my sense of what had happened to Roger's sleepy brain. He smiled and said to Debby. "Don't worry about Buster. I think he just took care of that black cat for good."

Bosley jumped up onto the foot of the bed and curled into a ball. Roger looked at him and Bosley smiled. He knew instantly that things had evolved in the Grand Scheme of Things. He purred softly as he fell gently to sleep.

CHAPTER 18

"Señor, Buster. Where did the evil black cat go when you pushed him into the black hole?" Jose asked, as the three of us meandered across the grassy hillsides of Green Valley toward the great gates that appeared on the horizon.

"I'm not sure, Jose. I think I pushed him back into the terrible ending of the Grand Scheme of Things."

"Is that what Harry designed as the great Apocalypse?" Bo inquired.

I nodded. "Yes. Everybody who is a part of it will experience great evil and chaos. It appropriate that Ace be there. Everyone will experience how time, and space, and stuff are all returning to their original oneness. I sure wouldn't want to be there."

Just as I finished speaking, a cobalt blue cloud again began forming overhead. It happened so fast that we all stood in awe as the mist swirled and congealed.

A voice boomed from inside the cloud. I recognized it instantly as the voice of the Creator.

"Buster. Good Buster. Your work is finally done. You've fulfilled all of the prophecies written in the book of Sampson. Now I can reveal to you a part of the grand scheme I did not share with you and Bo when we first met."

"What is that, Sir...er, I mean uh…" I was at a loss of words about what to call the Creator now that I knew 'He' was really a 'She.' Well, you know what I mean, Debby!"

I was embarrassed that I gave such a personal name and identity to the Creator. But She didn't seem to mind.

"Debby. Yes. That's a nice name. I like it. I don't mind being called Debby."

I think the Creator could see I was blushing, and I think She also heard Bo and Jose snickering. But it didn't seem to concern Her.

"What I didn't tell you, Buster, is that in the Grand Scheme of Things, there are occasional opportunities for some creatures to return through the Door of Light. And I'm going to give you and Bo such an opportunity, especially because your humans have not yet journeyed to the gates. Jose, you've got your human here already, so there's no reason for you to return."

"Thank you, Señorita Debby," responded Jose, as he bowed graciously and respectfully, as if in the presence of some grand lady.

I wasn't quite sure what the Creator meant. It sounded vaguely like the same promise that we just heard from the cat. It wasn't that I didn't trust the Creator. I just wasn't sure if there would be any "back there" for very long, now that the Creator had executed the Revelations Project.

"But Debby, haven't you started the Revelations Project? Isn't it designed to end the Grand Scheme of Things?"

"That's correct. The plan is completed."

"Well, doesn't that mean that everything will be gone when I return?" The Creator appeared to be amused, judging from the tone of Her response.

"Oh, Buster. You're such a thinker. Don't worry. Just because I started the program, that doesn't mean that it is instantly done. These sorts of things take a considerable amount of real time to complete. Goodness, don't you remember in the Book of Sampson, it took me almost a whole week of heavenly time to begin the Grand Scheme of Things?"

I nodded. That's what we learned in the manuscript Zack translated for us. It was also what I'd heard Roger and Debby discuss many years ago. Debby thought the Bible's version was supposed to be taken literally. Roger said it was just a metaphor. I thought to myself, why not take this opportunity to find out? I decided to ask the Creator Herself.

"Say, Debby. Would you clarify one thing for me? When you said it only took six days to create everything, were you referring to 24-hour human days, or some other type of day you measured by a different heavenly clock?"

"Buster, Buster. You've become quite the philosopher, I must say! I can see why your human Roger is so lonely without you. I'm not sure I can give you an answer that you'll be able to understand. Let me answer your question, therefore, with a question of my own. Think about this concept. Knowing what you know, if you were the Creator, how would you respond if someone asked you, 'How long does it take in human time to create a human?'"

I though about the question for a moment. Then I recalled that my human Debby told me it took nine months for Spencer to grow into his baby shape so he could be born.

"Nine months?"

"That's not correct. There is no measure of human time for how long it took to create Spencer, or any other human baby. It didn't take Me any time. I just caused it to happen."

I was confused. If it just happened, then why did it appear to take nine months to grow? The Creator could see I was confused. She tried another approach to clarify Her meaning.

"Buster. Everything that I have created was created out of nothing. Therefore, all of the wonderful stuffness of beingness is growing. When something is growing, humans need some way to freeze their understanding of it. That's why they created the measures of seconds, minutes, days, weeks and years."

As I thought about what the Creator was saying, things began to make sense. She was saying that the Grand Scheme of Things was like a baby growing. It was continuing to get larger.

"Do you mean that it is correct to say it took six days to create everything? Just like it is correct to say that things are still in the process of being created?"

"Precisely, Buster. You've got it! In human time, it actually didn't take any time at all to create everything. But if someone needed to describe a series of events, then it's necessary to use a time concept to help clarify it. From a human perspective, it took six days, because that was how the early prophets thought about time. Nowadays, scientists are more technical in how they describe creation. Many see it as an evolving, ongoing process."

Bo and Jose were sitting next to me, completely in awe because I was having such a philosophical conversation with the Creator. I thought it was great that She'd show concern for one humble dog, considering how small I was in Her Grand Scheme of Things.

"You've caused me to digress from my purpose, Buster, although I hope you'll find the wisdom useful. The purpose of my appearing to you is more practical. As I told you, I am preparing to return you and Bo to your former human owners."

I looked down at my perfect form, and hesitated to ask what I was sure would be perceived as a vain question.

"Excuse me, uh, Debby. Do you mean we're supposed to return to life? Isn't that going to be difficult?"

I looked at my great new form and remembered what I looked like the day Roger dragged my stiff dead body down the stairs. He'd buried me in a nice little grave in an animal cemetery. I was really curious about how all this was going to work. I'd seen some of those corny Grade-B horror movies where the ground opens up and out pops a dead body brought back to life. I couldn't imagine that Debby, or even Roger for that matter, would relish such an experience.

I must have been telegraphing my thoughts to the Creator. I thought I heard a gentle laugh, as if She were thoroughly enjoying the images that flashed through my mind.

"Take it easy, Buster. That isn't how it works. You'll go back as you are. I know how to do it. Trust Me. I've done it before. Now tell Me, are you ready to go back through the Door of Light?"

"Ready? Sure I am. Especially if I get to be with Debby and Roger again."

Bo was so anxious to return to Pam and Norm, he forgot whose presence he was in. He lifted his leg and made a great mark on the ground. "Oops. Sorry Your Highness Debby. I guess I got carried away," Bo said sheepishly.

"Jose, you've been an escort back through the tunnel before, haven't you?"

"Sí. You've sent me twice before. And I never told anybody, just like You told me."

"I know you can be trusted, Jose. So go now and take these two dogs back to their former lives. Then return as quickly as possible to your human, before he misses you."

Almost as quickly as it appeared, the brilliant cobalt cloud vanished, and the three of us were standing before the same kind of Door of Light that appeared in Debby's and Roger's bedroom at the time of my death. Jose led the way, his voice booming as he crossed into the light, "Come on, amigos, let's go! Geronimo!"

CHAPTER 19

When I emerged from the Door of Light, dawn was just beginning to break on the beach near the wall at Rio Del Mar. I looked around to see if anybody saw me, but there was nobody around except the seagulls and a few little birds scurrying across the wet sand in search of early breakfast.

"Wow. I'm back! I'm really back. I thought I'd never see this place again," I whispered to myself, as I walked around slowly and tried to experience everything all at once. There was the wall! It was like no time had passed and nothing had changed. It was like I was awakening from some grand dream.

I turned and saw another familiar structure. The Cafe Rio restaurant building, and the old mini-market paper racks where Roger used to occasionally buy a newspaper on our way home from the wall. There was one thing I needed to make sure about as I wandered around the empty parking lot. I just wasn't quite sure how to find out. Then it occurred to me. I ran across the lot and stopped right in front of the window of the restaurant, where I could clearly see my reflection.

"Great!" I wasn't in my old golden-white body. The Creator allowed me to return in my new, ideal body. An insidious thought nearly ruined my delight: was I just in another form of virtual reality, like in Green Valley, or was I really home? Now that I knew how the darn stuff worked, I would forever be suspicious of all this earthly stuff called reality. But I put all that cynicism aside as I walked around the deserted parking lot. For some strange reason, I felt the urge to run up the steep hillside above the level parking lot. I dashed out into the street. There was a screech of brakes and I realized that I'd just run out in front of a car.

Oh no, I just came back and now I'm dying again, without even seeing Debby and Roger, I thought to myself in alarm as the car squealed toward me. It stopped only inches from my face. Whew! As I opened my eyes, I could see that the person in the vehicle was hopping mad!

"You stupid dog. Don't you know you could get killed doing that? Where's your stupid owner anyway? You're not supposed to be here. You scared me to death. Don't you know I could have killed you?"

I stood there like a deer caught in the headlights of an on-coming car. Only this wasn't just any car. It was a blue Blazer, just like the one owned by Debby, and its driver had jumped out and was heading my way. Then I realized it was Debby's Blazer! This person was my human Debby! It really was Debby! My heart was pounding as she stomped toward me. I almost forgot that she was frightened and angry. It would have devastated her to hit any dog. Especially a Golden. I couldn't help smiling as she grabbed me by the fur behind my neck, probably thinking that I didn't have a collar. I was as surprised as she was when I felt her hand close firmly on the strip of leather around my neck.

I remembered that when I was at Zack's, he gave me the original leather collar worn by Sampson. Apparently I'd worn it through the tunnel of light, and it returned with me.

I smiled and tried to lick Debby's hand, as she led me to her Blazer. I couldn't help thinking how cleverly the Creator called Debby had been in arranging for my return. This was a class way to bring me back to my human Debby. But in the back of my mind, I wondered if she'd recognize me. I was also curious if this was the same scam Debby the Creator used to reunite Bo with Pam.

Debby leaned down and tried to see if there were any tags attached to the collar. There weren't. But the collar made her very curious. I heard her say to me, "Well, boy. It looks like you're owned by some hippie who's into Egyptian stuff. This looks like a really old collar. Somebody must really love you to have gone to all the work of making this collar. Come on, I'll take you home with me and we'll see if we can't find your humans. They're probably worried to death by now."

"Come on. Get in," she motioned. She was surprised at how quickly I jumped into the car and sat in the passenger seat.

It wasn't long before I found out that the Creator really wasn't very diverse in Her reunion strategies. After Debby made a few phone calls to see if anybody had reported me lost, she called her friend Pam. Before Debby could tell her what happened, Pam spoke.

"Debby, the strangest thing happened. I was driving down Freedom Boulevard early this morning and guess what happened? A young Bulldog that looked almost like Bo ran out in front of me. I damn near hit him. When I got out to see if things were O.K., he was just sitting there looking up at me and smiling, like Bo used to do. He didn't have any collar so I brought him home. Who would have thought in a million years that such a thing would happen? I've called around and nobody seems to know anything about him. I guess I'll put an advertisement in the paper. Norm's playing with him in the front room right now. He's already asked me what I'm going to do if nobody claims him…Hello, Debby? Are you still there? Is anything wrong? You're so quiet."

Debby's mouth had dropped wide open as she heard Pam's story. I was sitting right next to her so I could overhear everything that was said on the phone. I'd learned that trick many years ago. Debby was petting me in a loving way that must have connected her to past memories of me! I had on my very happy Golden Retriever smile. Finally Debby had the courage to speak.

"Pam, you're not going to believe what I'm going to tell you…" While Debby was talking, I looked all around the house. It felt great to be home again! I could hardly wait for Roger to get home from work. I expected he'd be home earlier because Debby called him and told him everything that happened. I knew he'd realize that this was part of the magic we'd both expected would bring us back together again.

CHAPTER 20

When Roger's Buick approached, I dashed from the balcony down the stairs and headed into the garage. The automatic door seemed to take forever to open. Roger was halfway out of the car before I hit him in a full run. I think I almost knocked the wind out of him. He'd never seen me with such a youthful, vital body. But I could tell instantly that he knew this different form contained Buster's spirit.

Roger bent down and ruffled my golden brown coat with both hands simultaneously. I licked his face all over. I could taste salt, so I knew he was crying tears of joy. They tasted so good! Then, as though it were the most natural thing in the world, Roger said:

"Welcome home, mule-kicker! It's good to have you back. We've been lonely without you. Let me say hello to Debby, and change my clothes. Then we'll go to the wall. What do you say to that, you old mule-kicker?"

"Hi, Debby. I'm home," Roger called as the two of us headed up the stairway to the living room. I waited impatiently while Roger changed into his familiar Oregon sweats.

"Come on, fella. How about running to the wall with me? Do you think you can keep up?"

I barked with delight as we made our way down the stairs and out the front door. I didn't especially like it that Roger stopped momentarily to grab the fancy retractable leash and one of my old collars from a dusty place near the door to the garage.

He kneeled down to put the collar around my neck, at the same time removing the ancient collar, which he examined carefully.

"I'll bet there's a very interesting story behind this collar, isn't there, mule-kicker?"

I licked his face and smiled. "You don't know the half of it, Roger."

It was at that precise moment that I knew Roger was sure it was me. He whispered into my ear, "I can hardly wait to talk with you at the wall, Buster!"

I tugged at the leash and headed for the wall at full speed. This time it was all Roger could do to keep up with me. I didn't even make any marks along the way. There would be time for marks later!

When we finally got to our place at the wall, it felt great to settle into our familiar positions. I felt as though eternity had passed since we first visited the wall. In a sense, it really had. Now we both knew that our conversations would be different. We both knew that the journey I'd made had changed things forever. There was so much I had to share with Roger. I hardly knew where to begin.

Roger began giggling like a child as he pulled the hood of the fading green sweatshirt up over his head to keep the cool evening breeze off his neck. He wrapped his left arm around my smooth and golden body. This was a new experience for him. He'd never sat with such a young Golden at this place on the wall. And, as he was about to realize, he'd never been with such a wise one either!

"So," Roger chuckled. "It sounds like you almost scared Debby to death when you ran out in front of her truck. That's not the way I'd get her attention. Have you ever seen the tail end of my Buick?"

We both laughed. Several years ago Debby's brakes failed when she was driving the Blazer behind Roger's two-week-old Buick!

"Do you think she has any idea that you're the same Buster that left here several years ago?"

Years ago? I was stunned. But I answered casually. "Yes, I think she does. She doesn't know what it is about me, or why she feels the way she does about me. But I'm certain she knows in her heart that it's me."

"How can you be so sure?" Roger was obviously not as convinced as I was about Debby's perceptions.

I licked Roger on the side of his face, and smiled my greatest Golden smile possible. "Well, it's very simple. When she got off the phone with Pam and found out about Bo's return, she got down on her knees on the kitchen floor and took both her hands and looked into my eyes and said, 'You're really Buster, aren't you? How on earth did you manage this new body? You and Roger have actually been communicating all these years, haven't you? Roger's not as crazy as I was beginning to think, is he?' Then she grabbed my body and held me close and sobbed."

"What did you do?" Roger inquired in a quivering voice. He was imagining how happy Debby was, at long last.

"Just to reaffirm her intuition, I raced over to a blanket that was folded neatly on the edge of the couch. I grabbed it and tucked it between my legs and wildly humped it like I used to do!"

We both laughed so hard that everybody on the beach turned and stared at the man in the University of Oregon sweats and the Golden, embracing each other as the sun sat softly on the deep blue ocean that stretched the full width of the horizon.

So, here I am, lying on the deck of Debby's house, enjoying the warm sun and the summer symphony of sounds and smells. Is this story true? Did it really happen? I can tell you one thing for sure. I did go through the tunnel. I did return through the tunnel. I suppose I should tell Roger to be honest when people ask, "How old's your dog?" If he wants to be truthful, he should say, "About twenty-four years' old," since I died the first time at twelve and here I am back to twelve again. Now that would make me at least 168 human years old! One other thought has stuck with me through all these strange events. Being here with Roger and Debby is all the Heaven I need. I have certainly learned that the wonderful stuffness of beingness is oneness.